Praise for Judith Eagle:

'A sweeping adventure ... echoing classic fiction from
The Secret Garden to Noel Streatfeild.'
Bookseller

'Absolutely sparkling, enchanting storytelling.'
Hilary McKay, author of *The Skylarks' War*

'A riveting adventure ... Eagle's writing grips the reader.'
Guardian

'A tour de force.'
Kirkus

'Eagle is a thrilling writer ... should appeal to boys and girls alike.'
Telegraph

'An absolute joy of a read.'
Emma Carroll, author of *Letters from the Lighthouse*

'Highly recommended.'
Pops, age 9, *Toppsta*

'Destined to be a future classic, Judith Eagle has all
the hallmarks of the next Noel Streatfeild.'
Scott Evans, *The Reader Teacher* & #PrimarySchoolBookClub

'A cracking read with superb storytelling.'
BookTrus

D1323267

ABOUT THE AUTHOR

Judith Eagle's career has included stints as a stylist, fashion editor and features writer. She now spends her mornings writing and her afternoons working in a secondary school library. Judith lives with her family and her cat Stockwell in South London. *The Accidental Stowaway* is her third novel.

ABOUT THE ILLUSTRATOR

Kim Geyer studied textile design before taking up children's book illustration. She lives in London with lots of pets and kids – her biggest inspiration. Kim loves ice cream and sherbert Dip Dabs and being taken for walks by her puppy, Dusty.

Also by Judith Eagle

The Secret Starling
The Pear Affair

THE ACCIDENTAL STOWAWAY

Judith Eagle

ILLUSTRATED BY KIM GEYER

faber

First published in 2022
by Faber & Faber Limited
Bloomsbury House,
74–77 Great Russell Street,
London WC1B 3DA
faberchildrens.co.uk

Typeset in Garamond Premier by M Rules
Printed by CPI Group (UK) Ltd, Croydon CR0 4YY

All rights reserved
Text © Judith Eagle, 2022
Illustrations © Kim Geyer, 2022

The right of Judith Eagle and Kim Geyer to be identified as author
and illustrator of this work respectively has been asserted in accordance
with Section 77 of the Copyright, Designs and Patents Act 1988

*This book is sold subject to the condition that it shall not, by way of trade
or otherwise, be lent, resold, hired out or otherwise circulated without the
publisher's prior consent in any form of binding or cover other than that in
which it is published and without a similar condition including this condition
being imposed on the subsequent purchaser*

A CIP record for this book
is available from the British Library

ISBN 978-0-571-36312-4

FSC
www.fsc.org
MIX
Paper from
responsible sources
FSC® C171272

2 4 6 8 10 9 7 5 3

For Moira, with much love.

RMS GLORIOUS

THE LARGEST, FASTEST AND MOST MAGNIFICENT STEAMER IN THE WORLD

Boat Deck — `1` ... `2`
Promenade Deck — `6`
Shelter Deck — `10` ... `7`
Upper Deck — `10` ... `13` `14` `1`
Main Deck — `16` ... `18` `7`
Lower Deck — `19` `20` `21`
Orlop — `22`

1. *Verandah Cafe*
2. *Library & Music Rooms*
3. *First Class Lounge*
4. *Grand Entrance*
5. *Bridge*
6. *First Class En Suite*

7. *First Class Cabins*
8. *Patch & Lillian's Cabin*
9. *Regal Suites*
10. *Second Class Cabins*
11. *Upper First Class Dining Saloon*
12. *Purser's Office*

13. *Pantry*

14. *Kitchen Galley*

15. *Lower First Class Dining Saloon*

16. *Third Class Cabins*

17. *Third Class Dining Room*

18. *Second Class Dining Room*

19. *Mail Room*

20. *Crew's Quarters*

21. *Stores*

22. *Cargo*

23. *Boiler Rooms*

24. *Baggage*

RMS *Glorious*

THE LARGEST, FASTEST AND MOST MAGNIFICENT STEAMER IN THE WORLD

LONDON TO NEW YORK

Sails at 4.00 p.m.

(weather and circumstances permitting)

Monday, March 7th, 1910

SALOON, SECOND CABIN AND THIRD-CLASS FARES STILL AVAILABLE

ACROSS THE ATLANTIC IN LESS THAN 5 DAYS!

Apply to

THE CUNARD STEAMSHIP COMPANY LTD

93 Bishopsgate Street EC and

29–30 Cockspur Street, SW, LONDON

Head office: 8 Water Street, Liverpool, England

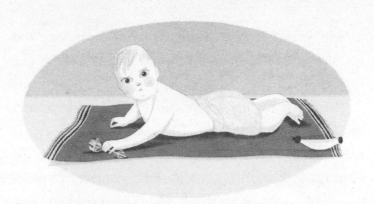

Chapter One

Right from the start she was known as 'Crosspatch'. Her real name was Esme Leonard but no one ever called her that.

In the London hospital where she had been born, it was a doctor who observed she should win a medal for grumpiness. The nurses raised their eyebrows but, in all honesty, they agreed. The baby never gurgled but always frowned! And no matter how much they tickled and cooed, her cross little face remained resolutely crumpled.

'Crosspatch needs her nappy changing!' they'd call to one another.

'It's time for Crosspatch's bath!'

'My word,' they'd laugh, as though it was the funniest thing in the whole wide world, 'look at the face on that!'

Over time the name was shortened and, like a label on a parcel, it had stuck. To make matters worse, it seemed like Patch *was* a parcel. Not a fancy one, all done up with shiny paper and ribbons; more of a plain brown one, with paper that has been used several times. The kind of parcel that no one wants to receive and everyone is always passing on.

'They tell me you are impossible,' Mr Ringe would say, and her heart would give a little thud.

'A ruffian.' Thud. Thud.

'A wild animal.' Thud. Thud. Thud.

Mr Ringe was the craggy-faced, somewhat gaunt solicitor in charge of securing Patch a home.

Passed from pillar to post, that was how *she* saw it. Her mother had run away when she was born; her father had died ages ago of something to do with weak lungs. She couldn't remember either of them. These were just the plain, hard facts.

Her journey had started in her father's three-storey house in Kensington, with a nursery at the top and a kitchen at the bottom. She had since been delivered to an aunt in Surrey, a grandmother in Northumberland, an uncle in Essex, and a second-cousin-twice-removed in Islington.

The aunt's house had been like a palace, with horses and stables and butlers in uniform. The grandmother had lived in less majestic circumstances, but that didn't stop her endless fussing about manners and etiquette. Then there had been the uncle, who practised a kind of godly austerity in his rambling vicarage. And finally the second-cousin-twice-removed, a most disgruntled individual who lived in a flat in a mansion block with only one maid and a measly allowance.

It was a bit like descending a very long staircase, the advantage being that along the way Patch had acquired an array of skills: she could ride a horse; she knew exactly what cutlery to use at a six-course dinner; she could stretch a chicken to make it last for several meals (the trick was to boil it and serve it with suet pudding); and she could unravel a whole jumper and (with just one extra ball of wool) knit it back together again a size or two larger.

Her downfall were the scrapes she was always getting into, not, *she* thought, all of her own making.

The aunt's children – spoiled boys, all three of them – had insisted on calling her 'No-mama' and in the end there was nothing to do *but* punch them.

The grandmother had so many rules to remember it made Patch's head spin, the worst by a mile being, 'You mustn't speak unless you are spoken to.' How on earth could Patch, who always had something to say, manage that? The uncle believed that little girls should only read Bible stories. So *of course* Patch had been forced to creep into the library at dead of night, frantically tear pages from the forbidden books and devour them in secret.

Unsurprisingly, Patch barely managed more than a few years in each place before being sent back to Mr Ringe.

'You have been found wanting,' he would say with an air of profound weariness, 'yet again.'

On her twelfth birthday the second-cousin-twice-removed declared Patch 'unmanageable' because she'd shouted at her in public, comparing her to a gargoyle and calling her a child hater. Patch was sent back to Mr Ringe with a long note full of grievances, ending with the declaration that the second-cousin-twice-removed never, ever wanted to see the child again.

'Well,' announced Mr Ringe, pulling despondently at his right ear, which Patch couldn't help noticing was fractionally larger than his left one, 'I would've preferred a bit more notice. While we await instructions, temporary arrangements will have to be made.'

'Instructions' were something Mr Ringe often alluded to. Who made them, or where they came from, was a mystery that was never shared with Patch. Patch stared hard at the solicitor and he stared back. Hard stares were one of her specialities. Mr Ringe blinked first and awarded her one of his historically long sighs. 'The thing is, young Patch, we have quite run out of relatives.'

It was Meg, the second-cousin-twice-removed's maid-of-all-work, who came to the rescue. Meg was the sort of person who left little cakes in Patch's pockets when she was sent to bed without any tea, and, more than a few times, she'd lent Patch her comics. The comics were full of adventure and derring-do – about girls just like Patch, but with better luck, who became top-notch spies or ran away to join the circus.

'A girl like that, in a home like ours?' Meg's mother had said when she had been sent for. Mrs Jenkins didn't mean to sound rude but she was a practical woman. Life in Lambeth was rough and tumble. She wasn't sure if this odd little girl would survive.

'Patch will be fine,' said Meg firmly. 'She's as tough as old boots, aren't you Patch?'

'I am,' Patch agreed, looking down at the lace-up boots peeping out from under her red dress. She clicked the heels together twice and tapped the toes. It was the sort of 'theatrical gesture' that would have driven the second-cousin-twice-removed mad. It was true that Patch *did* have quite fervent theatrical ambitions.

'And Mum won't be out of pocket, will she Mr Ringe?' asked Meg.

'A stipend will be paid for the girl's board and lodging,' concurred the cadaverous gentleman, and Patch saw, quick as lightning, the doubt in Mrs Jenkins's eyes disappear.

And it *had* been fine. More than fine.

Patch was adaptable. You had to be if you were a parcel, constantly being passed from pillar to post. Soon she had added to her repertoire of skills: talking pure cockney like she had been born to it, zooming around on one roller skate, which was all the rage, and minding Mrs Jenkins's youngest – who didn't seem to have a name; everyone just called it Baby – on one hip like the other girls in the street.

At the Jenkinses' there wasn't time to be cross. Even if she had been, they probably wouldn't have noticed.

Still, Patch was careful not to get too attached. She knew that once 'instructions' had been received, a new summons would arrive.

And it did.

Mr Ringe's brief note, delivered by the postman as Patch was gobbling down her breakfast bread and dripping, hinted that it was time for the parcel to be posted on. And when she arrived at the solicitor's office later that day, he wasted no time in delivering his news, rapping out the words in a tense staccato.

'Instructions have been received. You are to go to a friend. A *family* friend. Teaches at a girls' school. In Liverpool. Says she'll take you in. Best you can hope for. Given the circumstances.'

'Who sends these Instructions?' asked Patch, her face growing hot. A family friend? Who she'd never heard of? It sounded suspicious. She didn't trust the idea for one minute.

'Ask me no questions and I'll tell you no lies,' said Mr Ringe at his most infuriating. It was no good arguing; Patch had tried before and always got nowhere. So instead she kicked the solicitor's desk leg hard and watched a pile of probably very important papers fall with a satisfying thud to the floor. They looked like they had landed in a terrible muddle. Good.

She wanted to shout that she already knew this friend of her mother's would soon get fed up and pass her on like everyone else. She wanted to tell him that it was probably best if they just let her take care of herself.

But instead she put on her crossest face, a scowl of the highest order, just so Mr Ringe didn't forget who he was dealing with. Then she nodded and squared her shoulders. She would bid farewell to the dear Jenkinses. She would go to Liverpool, to this 'family friend'. She would try to be a pupil at the school just as proposed.

Because Patch Leonard was brave as well as cross. A survivor, just like the girls in the comics.

And anyway, deep down inside her leather boots her feet were starting to itch.

A train journey. A new city.

A teeny, tiny part of Patch actually quite liked being on the move.

Chapter Two

On the day of travel, Patch was up early. The train left Euston at eight o'clock sharp, and *whatever happened*, Mr Ringe had said, she mustn't be late. Patch wondered what kind of terrible happenings the solicitor might be imagining: fire, floods, plague or perhaps something more ordinary like mumps, which she'd had last year? It had been awful. Her face had swollen up so terribly she'd looked like a hamster and had to be confined to bed for two weeks.

Thankfully, nothing dreadful *did* happen and when the littlest Jenkins woke her up at dawn, there was just enough time to cram in a slice of bread and jam (a treat instead of dripping, said Mrs Jenkins, because Patch would need ballast for the journey), and after a round of hugs (and a few tears from Meg and Mrs Jenkins) she was off, marching into the grey morning light, lugging her carpet bag along beside her.

The bag weighed a ton and kept thwacking against her legs. It was stuffed to the gills with all her worldly goods: two chemises, two petticoats, her indigo dress, her plaid dress, two smocks, two knitted jumpers and a couple of pairs of black stockings. In the little space that was left, Patch had squeezed in a single roller skate, three issues of her favourite comic, *Girls' Best Friend,* and an extremely dog-eared copy of *A Little Princess*.

The days of hansom cabs were long gone, Mr Ringe had explained. There was no more money for what he called 'fripperies'. Instead he had provided Patch with a purse containing a few coins, and given her instructions about trams, tickets and trains.

As Patch wended her way towards Westminster Bridge, the day clattered along as though nothing out of the ordinary was happening. The streets were full of carts and coal lorries, rattling and banging; the fruit seller cried out her wares in such thick cockney it sounded like a foreign language; a barrel organ on the corner bashed out its cheerful tune.

At Whitehall, Patch hoisted her bag onto the

omnibus and in no time at all arrived at the railway station. She purchased her ticket, spent a few happy minutes listening to the man playing his fiddle by the station entrance, and then, when the guard called 'all aboard', leapt onto the Liverpool Lime Street train.

As the train whistled and wailed and left the station in great billowing puffs of steam, Patch dug around in her bag and fished out a copy of *Girls' Best Friend*. She'd intended to finish the story she had started the night before, about a 'boy' acrobat who suddenly turned out to be a duchess-in-waiting, but she soon became distracted and, instead, glued her forehead to the window and watched as the train sped past the backs of London's brick houses, a patchwork of parks, the suburbs, and gradually – as the houses petered out and the town became country – fields and woods and ponds.

The journey was a long one, five hours in fact, but Patch was not bored. She didn't dwell on what might await her in Liverpool. She had trained herself not to think too far ahead. She knew all about disappointment – both her own and being a disappointment to others – so instead she concentrated on enjoying the journey.

The rhythm of the train, the clickety-clack of the

engine, the hiss of steam all delighted her. Everywhere she looked there were things to observe: outside, the ever changing landscape, inside, the other passengers. The person opposite her had his face stuck in a newspaper. There were the usual headlines: the King was ill again, this time with bronchitis; a gang called the Fifty Elephants had made off with thousands of pounds worth of jewellery from a department store on Oxford Street; and – Patch leaned forward, suddenly alert – was that her heroine, the Russian ballerina Anna Pavlova? It was!

Patch adored Pavlova. She was said to dance 'not only for the eye, but also for the soul'. Last year she'd performed at the Palace – the handsomest music hall in the whole of Europe – and of course Patch had begged to go, but the second-cousin-twice-removed had said no. Patch squinted, trying to read the tiny newsprint underneath the ballerina's picture. Something about arriving in New York to cheering crowds and how in two weeks' time she was to perform a work specially choreographed for her called *The Dying Swan*.

Patch flung herself back in her seat and unwrapped the paste sandwiches Mrs Jenkins had packed for her. In the future, *she* would travel the world just like Anna Pavlova.

She could almost hear the rapturous applause. *Show your appreciation for the one and only Patch Leonard!*

One day people would adore *her* too.

* * *

When the train finally pulled into Lime Street Station, Patch was already on her feet, elbowing her way past the other passengers so she could be the first on the platform. For some minutes, she waited there expectantly. Then she walked in pigeon steps up and down the platform to kill some time. After a while, she unfolded the note from Mr Ringe and read it again.

> *Patch,*
>
> *You will be met at Lime Street Station by Miss Alice Grey, who forthwith is responsible for your board and education at the Liverpool Institute High School for Girls. You are fortunate indeed to have been offered this opportunity. Do not waste it.*
>
> *Mr R. Ringe.*

Patch crumpled the note up and stuffed it back in her bag. She was used to people not keeping their word. But still . . . Had this Miss Alice Grey decided to discard the parcel before it had even been collected?

Sighing, she picked up her bag, which suddenly seemed to have got a few tons heavier.

There was nothing else for it. She would have to make her own way there.

* * *

The Liverpool Institute High School for Girls was housed in an imposing-looking red-brick building. Patch stopped by the entrance and dropped her bag. She half expected a herd of girls to come rushing out, brandishing straw hats and hockey sticks. But it was deadly quiet. There was not even a whisper of chatter, no bells chimed announcing lessons and the playground was empty, apart from a scuffed tennis ball. Patch stooped to pick up the ball and hurled it hard against the brick wall.

'Esme Leonard from London!' cried a stout woman emerging from a door to the side of the building. 'You found your way here!' She plucked up the carpet bag as though it was as light as a feather and smiled broadly. 'I'm Mrs Blakeney, School Housekeeper, pleased to meet you.'

'I was meant to be met,' said Patch crossly.

'That's as may be,' said Mrs Blakeney, 'but I'm afraid Miss Alice had to pop across to Birkenhead on urgent business . . .' She paused and hefted the carpet bag onto her shoulder. 'It's her mother, you know, always calling on the poor soul to do this, that and the other. Anyway, I've got the gas lamps on and a fire going, and there's some bits and pieces set out for luncheon. I expect you're famished after your journey. Do come this way.'

Patch followed the homely figure up the stairs, along a corridor and up another narrower flight of stairs.

'Where *is* everyone?' she asked. It was so quiet it was like a ghost school.

'Why, it's the Easter break! Did no one tell you? Term doesn't start for two more weeks.'

Miss Alice Grey's rooms were right at the top of the building. The housekeeper showed Patch to her bedroom first, plonking the carpet bag down on the bed, and then led the way to the parlour. In the early afternoon light, the gas lamps flickered, turning the pale green walls the colour of rosy apples. Two velvet chairs sat either side of the fireplace, and in the grate a small fire burned. It was a perfectly lovely room that promised comfortable, companionable times, but it was the large window that made Patch gasp. It framed a view that stretched right across the city, all the way down to a cluster of masts and funnels on a river even wider than the Thames.

'The docks,' Mrs Blakeney explained, as Patch pressed her face against the glass. 'They call the ships "floating palaces", on account of them being so grand. They sail all the way across the ocean to the United States of America and back.'

Images of fairy-tale palaces with towers and turrets bobbing about on the sea filled Patch's head. She had read all about the ocean liners in Meg's magazines; some of them were as long as the Houses of Parliament, with tier upon tier of decks like wedding cakes, and palm courts, and orchestras, and daily newspapers actually printed at sea.

'Now here's your lunch,' said Mrs Blakeney, indicating a small table on which were set a plate of bread and butter, some slices of ham and cheese, and a wedge of apple pie. 'Eat up and unpack your things, and Miss Alice will be back for supper.'

After Mrs Blakeney had gone, Patch bolted down some bread and cheese and then took a tour of her surroundings. On Miss Alice's bookshelf was the exact same edition of *A Little Princess* that Patch had packed in her bag.

'Poor soul,' Mrs Blakeney had said about Miss Alice. But Patch decided she would reserve judgement. Miss Alice had told Mr Ringe that she would meet Patch at the station. She hadn't.

Opposite the bookshelf was a mantelpiece crammed with colourful postcards, a collection of shells, some dolls-house furniture made out of acorns, and a small package tucked between a bowl of potpourri and a china miniature of Jemima Puddle-duck.

'For E,' it said on the front. Patch plucked it up. It wasn't heavy. It was about the weight of a large conker.

Who was E?

Patch didn't often get presents. At birthdays, the aunt's boys got masses, the nursery a frenzy of discarded paper and piles of toys. She traced the outline of the E with her fingertip. Although she thought of herself as a P, strictly speaking she was an E.

Surely there was no harm in having a quick look? A grown-up would be bound to say no, but Patch didn't often do as she was told.

Quickly, she tore away the wrapping paper. Inside was a small turquoise box. She flipped it open. Nestling on a cushion of crimson velvet was the prettiest ring she had ever seen: a simple gold band set with a pea-sized ruby.

It was too big for any of her fingers but on her thumb it was almost snug.

'My ring!' she declared in her deepest, most actressy voice, wafting her hand about so that the dark red stone flashed enticingly. She imagined she was a long-lost heiress, perhaps a duchess, or a princess. 'At last, I've found my ring! Now they'll know me for who I really am!'

Snapping the empty box shut, she tucked it into the pocket of her red dress for safe keeping. She'd just wear the ring for a few minutes and then wrap it up again and pop it back on the mantelpiece. Still in character, she swept across the parlour and into the little bedroom, where she picked up her carpet bag and tipped the contents out onto the bed.

There was a clatter and a whirr and a second roller skate tumbled out on top of the first one. In an instant, Patch was back in the here and now. The dear Jenkinses must have put an extra one in! *No one* in Lambeth owned a whole pair of roller skates; they were a luxury, to be shared out.

Patch glanced up at the clock. It was only half past two. She picked up one of the roller skates and spun the wheel. It made a satisfying whirring sound. Was she really expected to hang around indoors all afternoon?

This Miss Alice would probably be out for hours. There was plenty of time to go for a spin. Take a closer look at those floating palaces.

Quickly, she buckled the skates on over her boots, and hobbled down the stairs, taking care to cling onto the banister so the skates didn't suddenly whoosh out from beneath her. Downstairs all was quiet. Good. No sign of Mrs Blakeney. She'd just quietly slip out and be back in a trice.

Outside, Patch whizzed across the playground, dodged the tennis ball, and swept out onto the street. Down she went in the direction of the river, each foot taking its turn to sweep forwards, sweep, swoop, sweep swoop, sweep swoop. When she was skating she forgot about everything. She was Queen of the World: just her, and the speed, and the world rushing by. The skates rattled and whirled, her skirt billowed out behind her, and her arms swung rhythmically from side to side, propelling her forwards.

She didn't see the bump in the kerb until it was too late, and then she was flying through the air, her arms scrabbling uselessly, and – ouch – she landed with a painful thud on the cobbled pavement.

'Whooaah!' someone cried. 'Would you take a look at that!'

Chapter Three

Patch didn't move. For a fleeting moment she wondered if she should just play dead to avoid the embarrassment. But then a face loomed in front of her, a thin face, with a sharp nose and quizzical eyebrows. Patch shut her eyes, but when she opened them again, the face was still there. It belonged to a boy and he looked as though he was about her age.

'It's rude to stare,' said Patch crossly, reaching for a nearby lamp post and hauling herself up. Her elbow hurt and her knee throbbed, but she wasn't going to let him know that. The boy wore a blue cap and a white kerchief knotted jauntily at his neck. His jersey had some sort of lettering on the front. She squinted at it while he stared unabashedly at her roller skates. It spelled out the word 'CUNARD'.

'Well pardon me for caring!' he said, tearing his eyes away from the skates. His accent was strange. The words seemed to roll off his tongue, as if they were curved.

'What sort of a voice is that?' she asked. The words popped out before she could stop them. She didn't always *mean* to be rude. She was just curious.

'Gee. Whaddaya mean what sort of a voice is that?! Didn't your Mama teach you how to talk nice?'

'I don't *have* a Mama,' Patch said stiffly. 'Not that it's any of your business. The way you speak. It's peculiar.'

'Well it ain't peculiar in New York,' he said. The way he said it sounded like 'Noo Yawk'.

'You're an American!' she burst out, her standoffishness evaporating. The boy must have crossed the occan in one of the floating palaces. 'Have you come off a ship?'

'Go to the tawp of the class!' he laughed and held out his hand. 'Arturo,' he said, 'Turo to my friends. I'm just off the *Glorious*, or the *Glory* as we like to call it.' He pointed at the lettering on his sweater. 'It's one of the Cunard liners. Came ashore to find a candy store. I could murder some – whaddaya English call it – tawfee. Know anywhere good?'

23

'No,' said Patch. 'I don't know a thing about Liverpool...but...' A thought struck her. Here was a chance to find out first-hand about the floating palaces. Were they really as grand as they said they were? And what was it like to be at sea?

Her mind made up, she sat back down on the kerb, and began to unbuckle her right skate. She'd noticed how he admired them. They could be her bargaining tool. 'I can easily help you find a sweet shop though. Want to share? I'll take the left one, and you can take the right.'

Turo's face broke into a grin. 'I sure do!'

Turo's feet were a little bigger than hers but, using the tiny key that was taped to the inside of the skate, Patch adjusted it to the right size. When he was ready, they set off, setting a kind of rhythm as they rolled and stepped, rolled and stepped, side by side.

'Are you here for a holiday then?' asked Patch politely, thinking how incredibly rich he must be. Although to be honest, he didn't have the air of a rich person.

'I'm not on vacation!' Turo burst out laughing. 'Do I look like a passenger? Nah, I work on the ship.'

'Oh!' Was he a runaway then? She'd been tempted to run away herself several times. The girls and boys in her comics were always scarpering off to sea to seek their fortunes.

'What kind of work?' she asked.

'A bit of everything,' he said grandly. 'Scrub and hose down decks, clean portholes, paint cabins, run errands for the stewards, keep the crew's quarters spick and span. They call me "the boots".'

Turo glided ahead of her and stuck one leg out behind him, arms outstretched as though he was skating on ice. He was better at skating than anyone in Lambeth. 'And I mean, SPICK and SPAN,' he yelled back over his shoulder, "cause the chief steward and the doctor inspect them every single day to check they're up to scratch.'

'Aren't you a bit young to be working at sea?' asked Patch as she caught up with him.

'Nope. They take you on at fourteen,' said Turo, executing a little twirl. He grinned at her, and he seemed as joyful and free as the birds that swooped and soared in the sky above.

'*Are* you fourteen?' asked Patch. She thought he wasn't. He was a gangly lad, but he didn't look that old.

'Not yet,' admitted Turo. 'But everyone knows that no one checks.'

'But what about your family?'

'Gee, you sure ask a lot of questions!' said Turo, laughing.

Patch stopped. 'Well don't answer them then!' she said hotly. 'You can give me back the skate and find the sweet shop on your own for all I care ...'

'Hey, no need to chew me out!' he said, and for a minute Patch thought that she had ruined it because people were always taking offence at her quick temper. But then she saw that he was still smiling, and she grasped at the smile like it was a lifeline and flashed one back.

'Thing is, there's an army of us at home, and not enough space and not enough dough,' he said. 'You should see us all, squeezed in like sardines in a can. On the ship it's another story! I have my own bunk, I get tips from the stewards and,' he patted his stomach, 'three square meals a day.'

Ignoring the indignant cries from a barrow man, Turo swiped two apples from a fruit stall, rubbed them on his sleeve until they shone and then tossed one back to Patch. She caught it and bit into it; it was crisp and delicious.

If he'd given her an apple, everything must be all right. Maybe he even liked her. She chanced another question.

'But ... don't you miss your family?'

He was doing zigzags now, his skating leg bent, his arms scissoring from side to side.

'I miss my mama's macaroni, and my papa telling us stories,' he said. 'I miss the *smell* of it – tomatoes and rosemary and lemon soap. And the sound of the traffic and the horses in the street below, and the taste of bread from Salvatore's . . . but . . .' He pirouetted round on his skate and grinned at Patch. 'I visit 'em every single time the *Glory* docks! And besides, I couldn't *live* without the smell of the sea, the whip of the wind and the toss and turn of the boat . . .'

It sounded like poetry, thought Patch.

'But . . .' she paused. Sometimes she asked so many questions people told her to shut up. 'What about seasickness?'

'Furgeddaboutit!' laughed Turo. 'Captain says anyone struck with it should lie down in the middle of the boat, starve themselves for two days and then drink iced champagne. Pardon my manners. I told you my name but you ain't told me yours.'

'Patch.'

She waited for him to laugh and make a joke about dogs or pirates, but he didn't. He just carried on talking, as though Patch was the most normal name in the world and as though she was a perfectly nice person.

'The thing is, Patch,' he went on earnestly, 'the more you're on deck, seeing the swell of the waves and feeling the rock of the boat, you kinda become one with the sea if you know what I mean?'

He *was* a poet, Patch thought. If she were at sea, she'd want to be a natural, just like him. Enjoying every moment, not feeling sick and having to lie down.

'Stop!' she called. She'd been so enthralled with everything he was saying that they'd nearly skated straight past a sweet shop.

It was small, on the corner, with a striped awning and a window display crammed with jars of bullseyes and liquorice and pear drops. Patch's mouth watered. She would've liked a quarter of something herself – vanilla fudge was her favourite. But she didn't have her purse. It was still in the jumble of belongings on the bed back in Miss Alice Grey's rooms.

Patch followed Turo inside, a bell jangling at the door to announce their arrival. Jars of Pontefract cakes, jelly babies and dolly mixtures lined the walls. On the counter a plate piled high with glossy brown toffee beckoned. The pieces looked like shards of glass, all jagged and uneven, as though they had been smashed up with a hammer.

'That sure looks swell!' said Turo.

'Why thank you. Made this morning, my love,' said the shopkeeper. 'Only a ha'penny for a quarter.'

Turo took his cap off and scratched his head thoughtfully, his eyes roving over the jars as though he was trying to make up his mind what to have. He glanced at Patch . . . and she recognised that look! It was the unspoken challenge of someone saying, 'Dare me?'

At speed, Turo threw his cap down over the plate of toffee, scooped it up, toffee and all, shouted '*Scusi*!' at the shopkeeper and 'Scram!' to Patch.

And then he was gone, the bell jangling furiously behind him, and in an instant, the shopkeeper had charged out from behind the counter and blocked Patch's exit so that she *couldn't* scram. There wasn't a hope of it.

The shopkeeper's face blazed an angry lobster red.

'Riff raff from one of them ships, no doubt, coming ashore and stealing my wares!' she said. Her eyes swept over Patch, taking in her shiny boots, her red dress. 'What's the likes of you doing with a boy like him? You'll have to settle up, come on, where's your money? Hand it over. You can make that a penny now for all the trouble you've caused.'

'But it wasn't me!' said Patch indignantly. 'I don't even know him!'

She'd seen the boys in Lambeth pull the same trick. Had Turo planned it? Had he meant her to take the blame? No. He'd said '*scram*'. He'd assumed they were in it together. But she hadn't been quick enough.

'Well, we'll have to get the constable along then, won't we, to see about that? He can escort you back to your mam and we'll hear what she has to say.'

'Oh we will, will we?' retorted Patch. She put her hands on her hips and stuck her neck out in a way the grandmother had said was threatening. Why did everyone always have to bring mothers into it? It made her blood boil. She could feel it now, roiling about from her head to her toes. 'And what if I haven't got a mam? How about that?'

The woman yanked open the door, put her fingers in her mouth and whistled. 'Constable!' she yelled. 'We've an emergency!'

Quick as a flash, Patch dipped her head, battered her way past the shopkeeper and out onto the street. Nobody was going to corner *her*. She'd show Turo what she was made of – and besides, he still had her skate!

The constable was already rounding the corner.

Making a sharp about turn, Patch shot off in the other direction, not back to the school, but after Turo towards the river and the docks.

Down the street she sped, swooping and swirling,

pretending she was a champion skater – no one could match her because she was the best. Behind her came shouts and the sound of pounding feet. Faster, she urged herself, faster!

Round a bend, past a trio of public houses, a couple of dining rooms, a department store – closing now, awnings being rolled up, steps being swept. On she went, twisting and turning, and then the tangle of lanes fell away, and ahead was a bridge, and on the other side of the bridge were crowds of people, all looking up and waving at a monumental ship.

Patch lurched to a stop. It was even bigger than she'd ever imagined, with four gigantic funnels painted a fiery red and vast twin masts stretching high up into the white-blue sky.

Beneath her red dress she could feel her heart hammering. And now she could see Turo! Pushing his way through the crowds, making for a sort of ramp. He turned and waved at her and then he was disappearing *up* the ramp. No, it wasn't a ramp, it was a gangway – and it was leading directly onto the ship!

The cheek of it! He wasn't even going to wait. She liked him, she liked him a lot, but not enough to donate him her skate.

Behind her, someone yelled 'Stop!' and she turned

to see a figure dressed in dark blue racing straight towards her.

Bother. The constable had followed her all the way here. There was only one thing for it. If she kept going she could dodge him in the crowd, find Turo, get her skate back and when the coast was clear, whizz back up to the school.

With a last burst, Patch skated full pelt across the bridge, weaving her way between the onlookers and then onto the gangway itself, the wheels of her skate whirring so loud they seemed to be buzzing. The sky disappeared and the side of the ship loomed black above her, and now there were more cries of 'Oi, come back,' and 'You can't go up there it's about to ...'

But Patch didn't stop. She ignored the shouts and the grumbles, skating further on, all the way to the top of the gangway, bumping onto the deck and then squeezing past more people – ladies in elaborate hats, men in suits, all leaning over the rail, waving handkerchiefs, calling goodbyes to the crowd below.

'What's that girl doing!'

'Who is she with?'

'Stop her!'

But Patch didn't stop. Something had taken hold of her – something unknowable, a kind of surge ... an excitement ... an urge to act and not think – and so she skated on, oblivious to the stares and shouts. This way. Round to the other side of the ship, crouch down, wrench off the skate, up a stairway and then out onto the top deck.

She could still hear the distant sound of the crowds cheering. But otherwise, all was quiet. She stepped across to the railing and peered over the side. There it was, the River Mersey. A great stretch of grey water, chopping and churning, getting wider and wider, on and on, until it reached the sea.

Patch let out a long breath. She had done it! She had dodged the constable. She was safe.

Except she wasn't because a moment later the peace was disturbed. She could hear footsteps from the stairwell she'd just raced up. And a voice.

She shot her head left, right. Turo and her skate would have to wait. She needed a hiding place.

All along the edge of the deck at regular intervals were boats suspended a little way above it. They were about the size of fishing boats, covered snugly with heavy canvas. Lifeboats!

Barely thinking about what she was doing, Patch leapt at the nearest one, dragging herself up, feet scrabbling at the sides, fingers tearing at the fastenings.

The rope was rough and scratchy but somehow she managed to loosen the ties, push back a corner of the canvas and scramble over the top. Hurling the skate ahead of her, she dropped down after it. Then she pulled the canvas back overhead.

It was dark in the boat and it smelled of oil and fresh paint and seawater. Patch scrunched herself up into a ball, breathing hard.

A giant boom split the air. And another. Two mighty blasts.

What did that mean? Surely the ship wasn't about to set sail?

In a panic, Patch jumped up and began to scramble back out of the boat.

And then, all of a sudden, she stopped.

It was now or never.

If she was quick – really quick – she could climb out of the lifeboat, race back down the stairs, tear across the gangway, and she might – just might – make it off the ship.

But, that would mean running straight into the arms of the constable. She pictured the hand, reaching out, grasping her by the scruff of the neck, and then the long, humiliating walk back to the school and Miss Alice Grey's inevitable look of disappointment.

She didn't want that. Miss Alice could hardly be expected to like her if *that* was her first impression. She'd probably give up on Patch right away.

It would be her fastest rejection yet.

And then Patch knew with every inch of her being that she'd had enough of being a parcel. She'd suffered twelve long years of being passed from pillar to post. Perhaps – the thought came to her, clear and sharp – perhaps, just for once, *she* could decide on her destination.

If she stayed hidden . . .

She could find Turo . . .

Get back her roller skate . . . and . . . take care of herself.

Another ear-splitting boom blasted the air. And then something mammoth began to thrum, vibrating through the soles of her feet all the way up to her chest.

Why shouldn't she sail to New York? Take in the sights, look up at the skyscrapers, ride the elevated railroads? She could even go to the Metropolitan Opera House and watch Pavlova dance *The Dying Swan*!

A thrill of excitement and absolute fear flashed through Patch's entire body.

The ship had begun to move.

Chapter Four

Patch pushed the canvas aside and hauled herself out of the lifeboat. The vibrating sound was everywhere, filling the air, barrelling into her ears, a deafening hum so loud it drowned out the cries of the seagulls in the sky above.

She sucked in her breath, her eyes wide as she surveyed the scene: the ship chugging its way through swirling waters, tugboats everywhere like tiny beetles, straining to pull the vessel away from the docks, downriver and out towards the boundless sea.

Part of her felt wild with excitement.

The other part was so scared she felt almost sick.

Now the ship had completed its turn, she could see the

docks and the teeming crowds again, a mass of cheering and waving. Somewhere out there was the constable wondering where she had got to. She shot her fist in the air, victorious. No one could catch Patch Leonard.

'Well, well, someone's feeling pleased with herself.'

Startled, Patch spun round. In a rush she caught a whiff of tobacco and expensive-smelling cologne, and at the same time a hand reached out and grasped her by the shoulder. It wasn't the constable. It was a distinguished-looking fellow with eyes the colour of sapphires and a cluster of grey-black curls. Several large rings set with glittering diamonds adorned his long elegant fingers. They flashed, almost blinding her in the late afternoon sun.

'Let go,' Patch whispered. 'Get off me.' What did he want? Had he been watching her the whole time? There was something menacing about him, something indefinable that made her recoil. He laughed, and as he did so, he released her, waving his silver-topped cane in the air. Then he turned and swaggered off down the deck.

Patch watched as he pulled open a door and disappeared inside the ship. Those cold, hard eyes had given her the shivers. In normal times she would have yelled after him to mind his own business. But now something stopped her. Had he seen her get out of the lifeboat? Had he realised she had dodged her way onto the ship? And what might he do if he had?

Quickly she clambered back into the boat and pulled the cover over it. What had she been doing, standing there in full view of the crowds! She'd have to be more careful.

And then she felt it: the ring, still snug on her thumb, pressing against her palm. She'd forgotten to put it back on the mantelpiece. *Stupid Patch!*

Miss Alice Grey would be home by now and she'd be wondering where Patch had got to. She'd call for Mrs Blakeney and she wouldn't know either. They'd search the rooms. They'd see that the little package was missing. They'd probably come to the conclusion that she was a thief.

Well, she wasn't. She'd never stolen anything in her life before. It was just finding the extra roller skate that had distracted her.

Patch stiffened. She could hear the sound of approaching footsteps. What if it was the horrible man coming back?

But whoever it was, was whistling. A jaunty tune, floating in and out amidst the cries of the birds and the noisy thrumming of the ship.

It didn't *sound* like the man. And he hadn't struck her as the whistling type.

Gingerly, Patch lifted the canvas an inch and peered through the gap.

It was a girl, scribbling something in a book with a stubby pencil, her yellow hair loosely tied with a ribbon, so long it almost reached her pockets. Somehow, she was managing to whistle and write at the same time.

As the girl drew close, a sudden gust of wind tore the canvas out of Patch's hands. Briskly it flapped up, and then down again, slapping Patch so hard on the head she yelped out loud.

The girl jumped and dropped the book. Cursing herself, Patch ducked down but it was too late.

'I already saw you, so you may as well come out.' The girl spoke quietly, as though she didn't want to be overheard, and yet her tone was strangely commanding.

Slowly, Patch stood up again and hoisted herself out of the boat. That was twice now that she'd been spotted. She wasn't doing a very good job of staying out of sight.

'What were you doing in there?' the girl whispered, glancing back over her shoulder. 'You gave me the surprise of my life. I nearly jumped out of my skin!'

She bent down to scoop up her book and brush the

dust off the cover; *50 Very Hard Crossword Puzzles*. Meg had liked doing crossword puzzles. Sometimes Patch had helped her with the answers. The girl saw Patch looking and popped the book into her pocket.

She was dressed most peculiarly, Patch thought, in an old-fashioned white dress with a giant blue sash at the waist. Her yellow hair gave her the air of Alice, from *Alice's Adventures in Wonderland,* except Patch was pretty sure that Alice's eyes were blue. This girl had coal-black eyes that were boring right into her, framed by the fiercest-looking black spectacles.

'I *said* what were you doing in there?' The girl had an odd accent, hovering somewhere between Turo's rounded vowels and Patch's more clipped, English ones.

'Keep your hair on!' said Patch, who was more used to being the cross one herself. 'There's no need to be so uppity.'

'Sorry,' said the girl straight away. Her spectacles had slipped a little way down her nose and she shoved them back up. 'I'm just interested, and ...' – she gave Patch an intent look – 'I can keep a secret.'

Patch stared at the girl. She wondered who in their right mind would entrust a stranger with a secret.

But then again, Patch didn't quite feel in her right

mind at the present moment. She couldn't be, to do what she'd just done, could she?

'If you must know,' she said, 'I got on by accident. The ship set sail and now I'm stuck.' She supposed that was the truth in some respects.

'What, so you don't have a ticket?'

'No,' said Patch. 'And you'd better not tell. If you do and they turn back, I'll ...'

The girl snorted.

'What's so funny?!' asked Patch.

'The idea that this ship would turn round and take you back!' said the girl. 'You must know the *Glory* will stop for no man, woman or child. How else will they keep hold of the Blue Riband?'

'What do you mean, blue ribbon?' Patch stared from the girl's face to the sash tied at her waist. She was talking nonsense.

'Blue Riband! It's an *award* not a *ribbon*,' said the girl as though Patch were a dunce. 'A ship is awarded the Blue Riband if it sails to the States in record time. Four days, seventeen hours and twenty-one minutes to be precise.'

So that was how long it would take to get there. Nearly five days. A long time to stay hidden.

'So, if you got on by accident ... and you don't have a

ticket . . . then you're a stowaway!' said the girl. She took a step towards Patch and clutched her arm. 'You know what happens to stowaways don't you?'

'What?' asked Patch, prising the girl's fingers open to release her grasp.

'Well, they *might* throw you into the jail right at the bottom of the boat and keep you there until we get to New York.' Behind the spectacles the girl's eyes gleamed.

'You're telling fibs! There is *not* a jail on this boat,' said Patch. Was there?

'There jolly well is,' said the girl. 'And if they choose *not* to put you down there, you'll have to pay your way, working as a skivvy shovelling coal or washing the decks.'

'How come *you're* such a know-all?' demanded Patch. The girl seemed astonishingly well informed.

There was a pause, and then she replied, 'Because I've sailed back and forth at least a dozen times.'

The girl regarded Patch for a few seconds and her expression softened. 'But for a novice, you've made a good start.'

'Have I?' said Patch, and she couldn't help feeling a flash of pleasure. She'd better not tell the girl that horrible man had already spotted her, or she might not be so impressed.

'It's a well-known fact that hiding out in a lifeboat is the stowaway's first choice,' said the girl authoritatively. 'They stay undercover by day and then come out to stretch their legs by night. And anyway, with all the comings and goings on board, it's really rather easy to get lost in a crowd...'

'But what about food?' interrupted Patch. She'd never be able to go five days without sustenance. She didn't want to starve.

'Not a problem,' said the girl firmly. 'The lifeboats are usually stocked with bread and water just in case the ship sinks – touch wood.' She darted over to the railing and touched it with two slim fingers. 'There should be blankets in there too.'

Further down, a group of adults burst out onto the deck. They were chattering and pointing to the sea. Patch shrank back into the shadow of the lifeboat.

'Quick,' said the girl. 'If you don't want to be spotted, you'd better get back in and stay there until it gets dark.'

For a second Patch bristled. She didn't like being ordered about. But the girl *seemed* to be on her side, glancing anxiously down the deck, and so she decided she'd better take her advice just in case.

Patch clambered back inside the lifeboat and was about to pull the canvas overhead when the girl hissed,

'Wait!' There was a scrambling noise and then in the gloom, Patch watched as a leg appeared, followed by another one, and then the rest of the girl presented herself. She flung herself down next to Patch.

'Fancy some company for a while? Budge up then and pull that canvas over properly. You don't want to give yourself away again— Oops, what's this?'

Something whirred in the dark.

'It's my skate,' said Patch. She reached out to take it, and as she did, she was suddenly aware that something was wrong, something to do with her thumb feeling all bare and—

'It's gone!' she said. Her chest felt suddenly tight.

'No, silly, I just told you it's here.' The girl shoved the skate at Patch, poking her with it in the ribs.

'No, my ring! It was on my thumb and now it's gone.' Patch scrabbled about in the dark. It was tiny! She'd never find it!

'Well, when did you last have it?'

'It was on my thumb a few minutes ago, I think . . . just before I saw you.'

'It can't have gone far then, can it?' said the girl sensibly. 'I'll start at this end and you start down there.'

Patch felt with her hands all the way along the base of her half of the lifeboat, searching inch by inch. She couldn't remember if she'd been in or out of the boat when she'd last felt it on her thumb.

'Got it!' the girl cried and Patch felt a rush of relief. The ring *seemed* important, as though she and it were connected somehow. She didn't understand why.

'D'you think it fell off because it's too big for you?' asked the girl. 'Hold on a minute, I've got an idea.'

Patch waited. There was something about the girl that was straightforward, as though she meant what she said. She heard a rustle and deep breaths of concentration.

'Here, lean over,' said the girl. 'I've strung it on my ribbon. That's it, I'll just tie it at the back of your neck . . . there!'

'Thank you,' said Patch. Her fingers crept around the ring, feeling its smooth band of gold and the facets of the ruby. She'd better not tell the girl how she'd found it. She might not be so helpful if she knew it wasn't – strictly speaking – hers.

* * *

There wasn't any bread and water in the lifeboat, but there was a blanket which they wrapped around them. The girl said she could stay until dinner time. Her name was Lilian and she surprised Patch by telling her she was also on her own.

'My parents aren't sailing back until next week. Mama prefers to travel alone,' she explained. Her mama was English and her papa American. That explained the peculiar accent, thought Patch.

'Is that allowed?' she asked. It was one thing to travel by train from London to Liverpool on your own. But on a ship, all the way across the Atlantic?

'Of course it's allowed! In theory, a stewardess is looking after me,' said Lilian airily. 'Not that she does much besides making sure I eat and sleep. But don't worry about me. I love my independence.'

'Independence. That's what I want!' said Patch, thinking how very self-assured Lilian was.

'Have you run away then?' asked Lilian.

Patch hesitated. A sensible person wouldn't blab. But Patch *wasn't* always sensible; she was headstrong, and she wanted to impress Lilian. Besides, she loved nothing more than an audience. And before she knew it, she was spilling out her whole story: her journey down the ladder, her short but happy time in Lambeth, and how she came to Liverpool. It was nice to be listened to properly for a change, instead of always being accused of telling tales.

Lilian asked a lot of questions. She wanted to know

everything about the aunt, the grandmother, the uncle and the second-cousin-twice-removed. She was especially intrigued by the Liverpool Institute High School for Girls. What subjects would Patch have studied? Did she like school?

When Patch got to the bit about skating onto the boat, she gasped.

'So there was no plan?' she said, admiringly. 'You just decided in that split second to stow away to the States? That's brave!'

In the darkness, Patch glowed. 'Like in *Girls' Best Friend*,' she agreed.

'I must say,' said Lilian, gripping Patch's arm again, and this time Patch didn't shake her off, 'I am glad you've come along. It's lonely on the ship without a friend.'

A friend, thought Patch. She'd not had many friends because she was always getting into arguments. And yet Meg had been one. And the Lambeth lot. She could do with a friend to help her survive this journey. And if she wasn't mistaken, Lilian seemed to be offering.

But still ... five days. Five days cramped up in a lifeboat and only coming out at night. Five days of relying on Lilian to bring her food and water.

It didn't sound like much fun.

In fact it made her feet feel quite itchy.

What she really wanted to do was dash all over the ship and explore every nook and cranny. She wanted to see all the things she'd read about: the fancy restaurants, the orchestra, the sweeping decks.

But what if those people who'd seen her running on board had told the authorities? What if they were already looking out for a stowaway in a red dress?

Unless . . . she twiddled the ring.

An idea came to her. It arrived fully formed. An audacious idea.

'Lilian—' she began.

But Lilian had sprung up and was pushing back a corner of the canvas. A triangle of inky blue sky revealed itself, punctuated by a single bright star.

'Don't go!' said Patch.

'I have to, sorry,' said Lilian apologetically. 'Esty – that's my stewardess – will be waiting for me. It's nearly dinner time. I'll bring you back something to eat later though, don't worry.'

'But listen! I've got a plan.'

Lilian stopped. Turned round. 'What kind of plan?'

'I'd like to come with you,' said Patch.

'But you'll be caught!' said Lilian.

'You said,' said Patch, 'that with all the comings and goings it'd be easy to get lost in a crowd ...'

Lilian sat down again. 'Yes, but I didn't mean ...'

There was a short silence. Instinct told Patch to wait. She sensed Lilian's curiosity.

'Well go on then. What *is* your plan?'

'I'm going to hide in plain sight,' said Patch.

Chapter Five

Patch told Lilian a story she'd read in one of her comics, about a runaway girl who fooled everyone into thinking she was a duchess.

'The thing is,' she said earnestly, 'rich people can do whatever they please.'

She could easily play the part. After all, she'd been a rich girl herself, first at the aunt's and later at the grandmother's.

'I suppose ...' said Lilian slowly, 'we could pretend I just ran into you on board and that our families are old friends.'

'Yes!' said Patch enthusiastically, thinking how lucky it was that she and Lilian had met. 'We'll have to invent a really important-sounding family name for me.' She cast around trying to think of something suitably impressive.

'How about the Cooper-Gordons?' suggested Lilian.

'I like that! And of course my house will have to be in Mayfair – that's where all the best London families live. D'you think it'll work?' she asked. 'Me getting lost in the crowd?'

Even in the gloom, Patch could see Lilian's eyes were shining, could feel her getting swept along.

'I do,' said Lilian. 'There are tons of people on the boat. No one looks very closely at children. Most of the time, no one pays us any attention at all.'

The first thing they did was swap dresses because common sense told them that if the crew *had* been alerted, they'd be looking for a dark-haired girl in a red dress, not a yellow-haired one. Struggling into Lilian's dress Patch nearly regretted it. It was horribly fussy and stiff, the sort of thing girls in the olden days would've worn.

'Good,' said Lilian, pulling herself out of the boat and dropping down to the deck. 'It's dark. Everyone'll be safely in the lounge now, having drinks before dinner.'

Patch jumped down after Lilian, landing with a thud. It was rare to meet someone who was almost as fearless as she was. In the red dress Lilian was looking less like Alice by the minute. She had a wicked grin and her black eyes flashed conspiratorially behind her spectacles.

Patch took a big gulp of salty air. She could feel the relentless thrum of the engines all the way from her feet to her fingertips. The sea was inky black and fathoms deep. Liverpool was far behind now. As Lilian had said, there would be no going back.

'On your marks,' said Lilian, and she darted towards a series of windows reflecting regular pools of light onto the dark deck.

'That's the lounge,' said Lilian when Patch had caught up with her.

Patch's eyes widened as she took in the scene through the window. Meg's comics *had* been telling the truth. The ship *was* like a palace. There were potted palms everywhere, and acres of panelled wood and yards and yards of Persian carpet; there were glittering candelabra and extravagantly corniced ceilings; there were even gilt-framed paintings of horses and hounds trotting across the walls. It was sumptuous, a cross between the aunt's mansion in Surrey and pictures she had seen in the grandmother's *Encyclopaedia Britannica* of Marie Antoinette's palace at Versailles.

'Down!' whispered Lilian fiercely, dropping to all fours so that she was out of sight.

Confused, Patch followed suit. And then bobbed up again for a brief last glimpse of the finery.

A weaselly-looking man with a ginger moustache was staring straight at her.

'Patch! Get down I said! Did anyone see you?'

'Just a man in uniform,' said Patch guiltily.

'Not a weaselly-looking man with a moustache and a terrible air of self-importance?'

'Maybe,' said Patch.

Lilian groaned. 'That sounds awfully like the new chief steward. Whatever you do Patch, *avoid* him at all costs. Now come on!'

Leaping up like a horse bolting the stables, Lilian turned sharp left and crashed through a set of double doors. Patch bounded after her. They were in a kind of entrance hall with a grand staircase sweeping away to the left and an electric lift at its centre.

Patch had been in an electric lift once before, in the newly opened department store, Selfridges on Oxford Street. She'd gone with the second-cousin-twice-removed, and she'd got 'lost' accidentally-on-purpose so that she could ride it up and down at least a dozen times.

Of course, she'd been punished. Sent to bed early without any tea. But still, it had been worth it. She'd loved the clang of the metal doors as they folded in on themselves like a concertina, and the whirr of the cables, and the buttons that you pushed to whizz up and down.

But just as she and Lilian were about to step inside, the doors to the lounge opened and a loud party of grown-ups spilled out into the hall, and into the lift ahead of them. In normal times Patch would've barged them right back. But now she used all her will power to restrain herself. She didn't shout. She didn't get cross. If she intended to hide in plain sight, she mustn't draw attention to herself.

'See?' said Lilian to Patch as the lift began to descend. 'How they completely ignored us? It's like we're not even here! Anyway, who cares about the lift? It's much more fun to slide down the banisters.'

* * *

'Lilian! There you are!'

Patch had followed Lilian along a bewildering set of passages, and now a woman in a grey dress with pristine white collar and cuffs appeared at a door to one of the rooms lining a long corridor.

'The bugler will call for dinner in fifteen minutes and— Oh!' The woman's gaze alighted on Patch. 'Who is this? And why is she wearing your dress?'

'It's Patch!' said Lilian. 'Patch, this is Esty. She's the stewardess I told you about, who looks after me on the crossings.' Lilian stopped and gave Esty a piercing look. 'Patch is on board with her family, the Cooper-Gordons. Mama and Papa are *such* dear friends of theirs. They visit with each other *all* the time in New York.' She ignored the question about the dress. 'And they want me to have dinner with them!'

Patch felt a bloom of admiration for Lilian. She had adapted to Patch's plan magnificently. She might even make a good actress herself one day. She definitely had what *Girls' Best Friend* would call 'pluck'.

'But Lilian,' said Esty, an anxious frown puckering her forehead, 'you always have dinner in your room. There's a tray ready for you and I'll be bringing it shortly.'

'Oh, Esty dear, don't look so worried. Now I've found a friend, you won't have to worry about me any more. Patch's parents invited me specially. Please say I can go!' She clasped her hands and gazed at Esty pleadingly.

Esty looked from Patch to Lilian and back again.

'The Cooper-Gordons …' she said faintly. 'Are you sure, Miss Lilian?' Patch crossed her fingers behind her back, willing Esty to fall for their story. The stewardess seemed to be genuinely puzzled. Perhaps she wasn't that sharp, as Mrs Jenkins might have said.

'Of course I'm sure,' said Lilian, a bit impatient now, turning to fiddle with the door knob.

Esty gave Lilian's back a searching look, and then turned to Patch. She seemed to be struggling to say something, but Patch didn't know what. She decided it was time to take matters into her own hands.

'My name is short for Patchouli,' she offered. 'After the perfume. Mama has bottles of the stuff on her dressing table at home.'

Lilian burst out laughing and Patch felt rather proud of her inventive thinking. Meanwhile Esty looked even more confused.

'Please don't worry,' Patch continued, 'my parents would be delighted if Lilian could spend the evening with us. Do say yes.'

'Very well then, I'll be back later to see you to bed …' the stewardess said reluctantly.

'You don't have to,' said Lilian firmly. 'Just tea and hot water in the morning, thank you.'

When the stewardess had gone, Lilian kicked the

door shut with her foot. 'It worked! Now, let's get you kitted out.'

While Lilian rummaged about in the huge chest at the foot of her bed, which had her name – Lilian de Haviland – painted on it in gold letters, Patch had a good look around the cabin. There were two single beds covered in peach-coloured satin quilts, with curtains to draw round them for privacy. There was an elegant chest of drawers and to either side of that, mirrored wardrobes. There was a washstand and a jug, a writing desk piled with books, and two easy chairs. It was all rather splendid.

'Does Esty sleep in here with you?' asked Patch.

Lilian laughed. 'No! Stewardesses have their own quarters. She shares a room with four others.' She found what she was looking for and held it up for Patch to inspect, a stiff-looking sailor dress with a white ribbon trim at the collar and hem. It was the sort of thing children would've worn before Patch was born. 'Will this do?'

It fitted Patch perfectly, even if it was a bit itchy. Lilian changed back into her Alice dress with the blue bow, and then crumpling Patch's red one into a ball, kicked it under the bed.

'Patch, you don't know how long I've dreamed about

dining in the saloon!' she said excitedly. 'I'm fed up of being hidden away down here all the time.'

'Hidden away?' said Patch. Lilian was rich. Her cabin made that obvious. Surely she could do whatever she liked.

'It's Mama and Papa,' said Lilian, taking her spectacles off and cleaning them on her blue sash. 'They worry about me all the time. They say they want to keep me safe. But it's so boring!'

'Grown-ups!' said Patch scornfully. The more Lilian talked, the more Patch liked her. Lilian's parents sounded positively awful: sailing on their own instead of with their daughter, keeping her hidden away in her cabin.

'They're so old-fashioned!' exclaimed Lilian. 'They haven't read any of the latest books about the new ways to bring up children.'

'Have *you*?' asked Patch incredulously. She only read story books and comics. Lilian seemed awfully studious. First very hard crossword puzzles. Now books about child-rearing. It sounded terribly dull.

'Of course!' said Lilian. 'And I know for a fact that children shouldn't be hidden away in nurseries. For our characters to develop properly we need to take part in rational discussions, be free, and do things like dine in the saloon if we want to!'

As if to punctuate Lilian's statement, at that moment a high-pitched trumpety sound rang out.

'The bugle!' said Lilian. 'At last.'

Patch linked arms with her new friend. She decided Lilian needed to worry less about things like child-rearing and concentrate more on having fun.

Maybe she could help in that department.

'Dining saloon, here we come!' she said.

Chapter Six

The dining saloon was spectacular, stretching over two floors, with the upper part in a gallery, so the passengers there could entertain themselves with the comings and goings on the floor below.

The girls stood for a moment, drinking in the splendour of it all. Everything twinkled – the glinting cutlery, the sparkling cut glassware and the spectacularly domed roof dotted with the signs of the zodiac, from which hung dozens of candelabra. An orchestra played and chatter filled the air. A rich place for rich people, Patch thought and couldn't help wondering what the Lambeth lot would've made of it. She could almost hear Mrs Jenkins sniffing and saying, 'It's not for the likes of us.'

'Matty!' Lilian had planted herself in the path of a waiter with hair the colour of a copper kettle, one arm aloft bearing a tray of glasses. 'This is Patchouli.'

The waiter glanced at Patch and then back at Lilian.

'Lilian, what are you doing in here?' He wore the same confused expression that Patch had seen on Esty earlier.

'Patch's family are the Cooper-Gordons,' explained Lilian hurriedly, nodding in the direction of the balcony, 'and they invited me to dinner and—'

'To dinner?'

'Yes,' broke in Patch, coming to the rescue. 'But there's no space at our usual table. Could you be a darling,' she added, a touch imperiously, 'and set two places for us down here?'

Lilian's face broke into a grin and her brows danced happily above her spectacles. 'You *can* act,' she whispered.

'Very well then,' said Matty, looking a little taken aback but nevertheless guiding them over to a central table, beautifully set with a snowy white tablecloth, an impressive arrangement of lilies as a centrepiece and a staggering array of knives, forks and spoons.

'There's two places here,' said Matty, looking up at the balcony as if for approval. 'Can you see your parents from here?' he asked Patch, glancing up again.

'I can,' said Patch graciously, fluttering a wave at an imaginary couple. 'Thank you so much ... Matty, was it? I'll make sure my parents know how helpful you have been.'

'You're good!' whispered Lilian as they sat down. 'Remind me what order to use the cutlery?' she added, keeping her voice low. 'They follow British rules on the ship and I've been brought up to dine in the American fashion.'

Patch hadn't known there were different rules on either side of the Atlantic, but she quickly pointed out the soup spoon, the dessert spoon and the fish and meat knives and forks. 'And always start from the outside and work inwards,' she muttered.

As the soup arrived, Patch examined the other guests. To her right sat an elderly lady with a head full of silvery platinum curls and tinted spectacles. Rather surprisingly for such a fancy dining saloon, a solid-looking white dog was sitting squarely on her lap. Patch said, 'May I?' and reached out and scratched his forehead gently. He eyed her carefully and she gave him a friendly smile. She loved dogs. She'd once found a stray and tried to smuggle him into the grandmother's. The maid had blabbed and the grandmother had had a fit. It hadn't ended well.

'Welcome to the outsiders' table.' The lady smiled, showing off a gold tooth. 'For the headaches,' she explained, tapping her spectacles. 'Terrible bad they are. Just one glance at the sun or electric lights sets them off something rotten. This is Sid. Say hello, Sid.'

The dog cocked his peculiarly egg-shaped head. He had pinkish eyes, a round, hard body and a pair of muscular shoulders. He sighed in such a way that made Patch wish she could scoop him up in a hug.

'Ah, the latecomers!'

Patch followed the elderly lady's gaze and stiffened. Lowering himself into the seat opposite was the man with the grey-black curls and piercing blue eyes. Placing his silver-topped cane on the table, he caught Patch's eye and smiled, his lips curling in a way that told her it wasn't entirely genuine.

Did he recognise her from earlier? Or was it just a polite greeting? Her instinct was to scowl, throw him a hard stare. But instead she forced herself to smile back.

He turned and whispered something into the ear of his companion, a young woman who looked as though she had stepped straight out of a fashion plate. She wore one of the latest picture hats crammed with flowers and birds and wafting feathers – the kind that would be infuriating if the wearer sat in front of you at the theatre. Green satin gloves were pulled up to the very tops of her arms, and a thick choker of rubies and pearls winked and blinked at her throat.

The man on the other side of Lilian stood up and clinked his glass with a spoon. 'I guess we should all introduce ourselves. Seein' as we'll be sharing a table for the next five days an' all.'

His name was Jimmy and he was a fine-looking chap, with eyes that danced and a dazzling smile. He was a composer, he said, and he played all the instruments but mainly 'pee-*yaaaaa*-nooo, not too badly – you can listen to me in the lounge later on.'

The whole time Jimmy talked, he clicked his fingers and tapped his toes in time to the band. 'I'm opening my very own club in New York!' he declared. 'I'm gonna fill it to the rafters with the biggest orchestra that you ever did see. There'll be fellas playin' drums and banjos, as well as all the usual horns and strings. Y'all be welcome any time.'

'Thank you!' Patch chipped in eagerly. She loved music and Jimmy's orchestra sounded marvellous. The rest of the table seemed a trifle startled by her enthusiasm but she didn't care. 'I'd love nothing more!'

'I shall look forward to greeting you there, young

Patch,' said Jimmy. 'And you, sir? What brings you to the States?' he enquired of the gentleman opposite.

'We're in the jewellery business,' the man drawled. 'Name's Reynolds. Delighted to meet you all.' He raised his glass and took a puff of his cigar. 'We plan to take Fifth Avenue by storm, eh Mrs Reynolds?'

Mrs Reynolds clasped a hand to her throat and bobbed her head in agreement, the embellishments on her picture hat nodding along.

'How lovely,' the elderly lady said brightly. 'I'm June Fortune and I'm very pleased to meet you all. Ah, thank you!' She accepted a menu from the same waiter, Matty, who had seated Patch and Lilian earlier. 'Now Sid, hows about we try you on something a bit more adventurous than ginger biscuits for once. What would you like?'

Sid cast a singularly unimpressed look in June's direction.

Ignoring the dog, June smiled gaily at Patch and passed her the menu. It was elaborately designed on pink card in a curly script. At the top it read 'For your little treasure, Madam' and underneath was a four-course menu, in French. It was a menu for dogs, Patch realised, and she was about to burst into laughter at the extravagance of it but was silenced by a fierce look from Sid. She didn't think he *was* fierce inside though. She suspected that beneath that tough exterior lay an extremely sensitive soul.

'*Côte de boeuf*?' she suggested. 'Or *pâté de foie gras*?'

'Excellent suggestions.' June smiled and handed the menu back to the waiter. 'Let's give the beef a whirl.'

'What did you mean when you said that about outsiders?' asked Patch, tucking her legs under her so she was kneeling on the chair and resting her elbows on the table. It was the most comfortable dining position in the world. All the relatives would have shrieked in horror. They were obsessed with silly rules. No kneeling, no talking with your mouth full, no eating with fingers.

But none of that mattered any more. She could do what she wanted now.

'Well,' said June, lowering her voice and indicating the rest of the room with a wave of her hand. 'Open your eyes, my dear! The Vanderbilts, the Astors, the Fricks. All wildly rich and all friends with each other. The odd ones out, that's what we are. Or at least I am, and I should think this here Jimmy is, what with him being a musician and ...' She trailed off as her gaze rested on Mrs Reynolds who was daintily eating her soup with her dessert spoon.

'May I ask if you two are on your own?' She nodded from Patch to Lilian.

'I'm with my parents, the Cooper-Gordons of Mayfair,' said Patch, tilting her head in the direction of the balcony. 'Lilian is on her own though, aren't you?' she said, elbowing her friend. Lilian, who had been chatting to Jimmy, turned and nodded in agreement.

'My parents, the de Havilands, are still in London,' she informed June. 'They're making the crossing next week.'

June, contrary to most of the adults Patch had met, *was* interested in children and asked a lot of questions, and Lilian joined in the conversation enthusiastically. Yes, she was travelling alone, with a stewardess for a companion, and yes, her family did live in a mansion on Fifth Avenue with fifteen bedrooms and an oak-floored ballroom big enough for four hundred guests. Yes, Papa was a banker. No, they didn't know the Astors yet but Mama had plans to invite them round for tea very soon. June listened avidly, and in return fed them London gossip. She tried to tempt Sid to his *Côte de boeuf*, but he turned his snout up haughtily, and in the end she gave up and fed him half a dozen ginger biscuits instead.

The evening passed in a whirl of poached halibut,

plum pudding and champagne jelly with ice cream. When it was over, the guests scattered, some to the library, some to the smoking room, some calling to each other to grab their coats and meet in the Verandah Café.

June and the girls followed Jimmy into the lounge, where he was introduced as 'the famous Jimmy Taylor, King of Ragtime!' to wild applause. It was wonderful, watching his hands flying across the keys playing some of the most joyous foot-tapping music Patch had ever heard. Even so, before long, her head began to droop and no matter how much she blinked, she began to fight a losing battle with her eyes, which were determined to close.

'I need to get back to my lifeboat,' she whispered to Lilian. The thought of its dark recesses, its smell of oil and fresh paint and seawater was all of a sudden quite appealing.

'No, Patch!' whispered Lilian, her eyes wide. 'We're in this together now – let's smuggle you into my room. You can hide out with me!'

* * *

With most of the stewards flying about ministering to the whims of the grown-ups – delivering after-dinner drinks, preparing hot water bottles, or fetching furs and blankets for those who wanted a late-night stroll on deck – nobody saw Patch sneak into Lilian's cabin.

'Oh, that was lovely, Patch,' declared Lilian, flinging herself onto one of the twin beds. 'I've dreamed and dreamed of dining in the saloon. And it was exactly how I imagined! Wasn't the champagne jelly divine?'

'But don't you do that kind of thing all the time in New York?' asked Patch, puzzled. Surely a family who lived in a mansion on Fifth Avenue with fifteen bedrooms and an oak-floored ballroom would be entertaining frequently.

'Of course!' said Lilian, looking a little flustered. She took off her spectacles, blew mist onto them and then wiped them on the corner of her dress. 'But I'm never allowed to join in. Mama and Papa insist on me keeping to the nursery. They say, "Soirées aren't suitable for children."'

Poor Lilian, thought Patch. No wonder she had been almost giddy with excitement at dinner.

'What did you think about the other guests?' asked Lilian as they climbed into bed with their dresses on because Lilian couldn't be bothered to change into her night gown and Patch didn't have one.

'I liked Jimmy and June,' said Patch. 'But the

Reynolds ...' She still hadn't told Lilian about her encounter with Mr Reynolds earlier. 'He's—'

'So distinguished,' gushed Lilian, 'and have you ever seen anyone even half as glamorous as his wife?'

Patch, who had been about to say that she thought Mr Reynolds rather sinister, stopped. Perhaps she was wrong. Part of her didn't trust him one jot. But he'd said nothing at dinner. Maybe he *hadn't* seen her get out of the lifeboat.

'But could you hear a thing Mrs Reynolds said?' she replied instead. 'She only talked in whispers! I did like her beauty spot though.'

'The mole above her lip, d'you mean?' said Lilian.

'Oh Lilian! All the papers call them beauty spots.' Lilian really was *very* unsophisticated, Patch thought. Leaping out of bed, she fetched a pen and a pot of ink from the desk. 'I'll draw one on for you if you like. I think it'd suit you!'

'All right,' said Lilian, leaning back and closing her eyes.

So Patch dipped the nib in the ink and very carefully tried to ink a dot above Lilian's upper lip, but it was hard with the constant thrumming of the ship and her hand slipped.

'I'll have to turn it into a moustache,' she said,

giggling, and before Lilian could stop her, she'd coloured in the whole of Lilian's upper lip with blue ink. 'There,' she said, and Lilian looked in the mirror and shrieked with horror and threw her pillow at Patch and Patch threw it back, and for a few minutes they fought riotously and uproariously until it suddenly dawned on them that the noise they were making might alert a passing steward to the illegal occupant.

When the lights had been turned out they carried on whispering. It was cosy in the room with the constant thrum of the engines.

They agreed that the next day they would find Turo and get Patch's roller skate back so that she could teach Lilian how to skate, and they could go whizzing up and down along the decks.

'Patch,' said Lilian, 'you know when you were in Liverpool? Didn't a little part of you *want* to stay at the school?'

'The Liverpool Institute?' said Patch. 'Stuck in a classroom all day? No thank you very much.'

She thought about her experiences of education: a succession of governesses at the aunt's, the grandmother's and the uncle's; a day school fixated on needlework at the second-cousin-twice-removed's. By far the best had been the local school in Lambeth. Not the lessons, but the breaks, where they'd played endless games of marbles and leapfrog and tag in the playground.

'Well, *I'd* like to go to school,' said Lilian. She sounded wistful. 'A proper one, where you learn proper things. Not just silly sewing, but French and Latin, and History and Mathematics.'

'Well, what's stopping you? Surely you go to school in New York?'

There was a silence, followed by a sigh, and then, 'It's not that simple, Patch.'

'But ...' Why couldn't Lilian go to school? Surely her parents could afford to send her to the grandest of establishments?

Maybe they were the sort who didn't believe in education for girls.

'It doesn't matter,' Lilian said. Her voice sounded flat and Patch could tell the subject was closed. She was probably embarrassed. Embarrassed about having such awful parents. Sometimes Patch thought she was blessed not having any at all. They could cause an awful lot of trouble.

She rolled over and hugged her knees to her chin.

She could barely believe that only that morning she had woken up in Lambeth. Never in her wildest dreams had she thought the day would end on one of the floating palaces. She felt for the ring hanging on the ribbon round her neck and rubbed its contours with her thumb and forefinger.

Had it been meant for her? *Was* she E? There was something about it that felt right. Lucky, even. Since it had been in her possession, she'd met Turo, dodged her way onto the ship and made a friend in Lilian. A shiver of anticipation flew up her entire body.

The plan to hide in plain sight was working. With Lilian's help she could travel all the way to New York undetected.

And when she got there, she would go straight to the Metropolitan Opera House. If she could stow away on a ship, there was no reason why she couldn't sneak in to see Pavlova.

Chapter Seven

'Wake up, Patch!'

All in a muddle, Patch opened her eyes. Where was she? What was that buzzing sensation she could feel vibrating through the mattress and up into her back and her chest? And then she saw Lilian's mass of golden hair and her beetle black eyes behind her spectacles and everything came flooding back.

She was at sea. Speeding her way across the Atlantic. She had run away from Liverpool and she was headed for New York.

'Patch!' Lilian hissed, pulling back the eiderdown. 'I know you're awake! Esty will be here any minute, you need to hide.'

Patch stumbled out of bed and into the cupboard-sized room that held the WC, wincing as Lilian kicked the door unceremoniously shut behind her. In the tiny mirror on the back of the door, her face, pale and crumpled, stared back at her, her almost-black thicket of hair sprouting out of its untidy plait. She heard a knock and then muffled voices. She put her ear to the door and strained to make sense of the murmurs and mumbles, but the vibration of the ship drowned everything out.

After a few minutes the door opened. 'Coast's clear,' said Lilian. She still had a blueish tinge above her lip where the inked moustache had been.

Besides a jug of hot water, Esty had left a tray of tea, toast and eggs – hard boiled and soft – which the girls fell upon as though they hadn't eaten for weeks. Afterwards, they took turns swigging tea out of the one cup provided while they worked out how they could get the skate back from Turo.

Lilian said that if Turo's job was to look after the crew's quarters, he would be right in the bowels of the boat. 'Below the water line,' she said. 'We can get the lift down there, but not when the stewards are around asking too many questions. We'll go when everyone's at luncheon.'

In the meantime, she would give Patch a guided tour of the ship. 'It'll be confusing at first, but when you get the hang of it, it all makes sense.'

They took the grand staircase, and as they climbed, Lilian explained that there were eight decks in total. 'Our cabin is on the upper deck,' she said, 'and below that is the main deck; below *that*, is the lower deck, and right at the bottom is the orlop deck where the engines and the cargo are.'

Patch swept her hand along the smooth, polished wood of the banisters. She imagined sliding all the way down to the orlop, which sounded like another world, an underground world manned by secret little people.

'Patch, are you listening? This is the shelter deck. Come on!' Ignoring the disapproving stares of the other passengers, they skidded across the black and white tiled floor to the next flight of stairs. 'And this,' Lilian said at the next landing, sweeping her arms wide, 'is the promenade deck. If we carried on going up, we'd get to the boat deck where I found you yesterday.'

As they pushed through a set of double doors, a blast of wind almost sent them backwards. It was the most glorious day. The sky blazed a piercing blue, and the silvery sea, tipped with frilly white lace, rippled as far as the eye could see.

'It's beautiful!' Patch exclaimed.

'You say that now,' said Lilian darkly. 'Just you wait. When the storms come it's a different story.'

The wind whipped Patch's plait into her eyes and her mouth. Her lips tasted of salt. For a brief moment the breeze dropped. The golden brown boards of the deck stretched away enticingly. It would be perfect for roller skating. Better even than a proper rink.

'Patch, listen!' Lilian shook Patch's arm. 'If that's the front of the ship,' she pointed beyond Patch, 'then which side of the boat are we on?'

'Left side,' said Patch, who was good at geography and directions in general.

'Right, but wrong,' said Lilian. 'It *is* the left side but on the ship we call it port. The right-hand side is called starboard. Understand?'

'I think so,' said Patch. She was trying to concentrate on what Lilian was saying but she was far more interested in the sea. The ship was going fast, churning its way through the water. It was majestic. Magnificent. It made her feel small and big at the same time.

'The front of the ship is called the bow,' continued Lilian, shouting so that Patch could hear her above the wind, 'and the back is called the stern. If someone comes up to you and says "forward deck", they mean the front part of the ship, and if they say "aft", they mean the rear part, towards the stern. Amidships is the middle. It's where there is the least vibration, where the lounge is, and the library and the music room and the dining room. For first class that is.'

'How many classes are there?' asked Patch, her head reeling with all this information. She'd never be able to remember it all.

'It's complicated,' said Lilian. 'The whole ship is carved up into first class, second and third. They like to keep us all separate. Look!'

She dashed over to the railing opposite, gesturing for Patch to follow. Patch joined Lilian and leaned over the railing. The deck below was busy with people. Children with chalk marking out hopscotch; a large family eating apples, spread out over several blankets; a group of young men sharing a joke; two young ladies in fits of laughter. Patch waved at a little boy doing cartwheels and he waved cheerfully back.

'And *can* they keep everyone separate?' she asked.

'If you know how, there are ways between,' said Lilian, grinning. 'Back stairs, one of the lifts, a hatch here and there. There are gates too, locked ones. But guess what ...?'

'What?' asked Patch. Lilian had a mischievous look in her eyes.

Reaching into her pocket, she withdrew something and held it up. A hefty-looking key.

'Where d'you get that?'

'Esty left it out and I took it,' said Lilian.

'So you can go anywhere you like?' asked Patch eagerly.

'Pretty much,' smiled Lilian, and her black eyebrows twitched in satisfaction.

They had reached a recess with a bench in it, tucked out of the wind, and they sat, their legs stuck out in front of them.

They talked for ages and it was delicious. Apart from Meg, Patch had not had much experience in the joy of conversation with someone she liked. Now the floodgates opened and the talk flowed forth. Patch told Lilian she was going to be an actress or a dancer when she grew up. She showed Lilian how she could spin and twirl like Isadora Duncan, and Lilian applauded as if it was the best thing in the world. Lilian wanted to be a scientist like Madame Curie. 'Or maybe I'll be a writer and write books about orphans, girls like you Patch . . .'

'But I'm not an orphan!' exclaimed Patch, twiddling the ring on the ribbon around her neck. 'I have a mother … somewhere. It's just … she ran away.' She didn't usually mention the fact that she even *had* a mother. But there was something about Lilian that made her talk, that made words just pop out before she could stop them.

'Can I see?' asked Lilian. She leaned over and plucked up the ring with her thumb and forefinger.

'Patch, who *are* E and E?'

'What?' said Patch. She didn't have a clue what Lilian was talking about.

'The engraving on the inside! You must've seen it!'

Patch yanked the ring out of Lilian's grasp and examined it. She almost had to go cross-eyed to decipher it from this angle. But sure enough, on the inside were two entwined initials.

E. & E.

Patch became aware that Lilian was observing her curiously. She was probably wondering why she'd never noticed the engraving before. Did she dare own up? Tell Lilian that she wasn't entirely sure if the ring was hers?

It would be a test, she decided. Of their friendship. If Lilian didn't like it, she could lump it.

'The thing is,' she admitted, 'I took it. From Miss Alice Grey's mantelpiece. It was in an envelope marked E and I thought—'

'But you're a P!' interrupted Lilian.

Oh dear. She wasn't going to approve, thought Patch.

'But my real name's Esme,' she added quickly. 'Although nobody ever calls me that.'

She stared at Lilian defiantly, steeling herself for the judgement that would surely follow. So what? She didn't care! She'd managed without friends so far.

But Lilian wasn't frowning, she was smiling. And she was nudging Patch in the ribs. 'Of course it's for you then!' she said.

Patch was surprised how relieved she felt. Relieved that she didn't have to break up with Lilian; relieved that they didn't have to have an argument, that they were still friends.

She squinted at the initials again, taking her time now that she knew Lilian was on her side. 'But it's a bit of a mystery, isn't it?' she said. 'Why would Miss Alice Grey give me a present? If it *is* from her. After all, *her* initial isn't E. It's A G.'

'What if . . .' said Lilian after a pause, 'it's from your mother? The one who ran away?'

Patch snorted. 'Not likely! I don't even know my mother's name. She might be an A or a B or a C for all I care.'

'What?' Astonishment was written all over Lilian's

face. 'Nobody ever told you her *name*? Didn't you *want* to know?'

'Of course not,' said Patch hotly. The conversation was beginning to go off in a direction she hadn't anticipated. And she didn't particularly like it.

'She didn't want me so why should I want her?' she said. 'The relatives never spoke about her. And anyway, what on earth has she got to do with Miss Alice and the school in Liverpool?'

Lilian opened her mouth to say something and then closed it again. A small squat thing with an egg-shaped head and stubby legs had bounded over to them. With a yelp, it started butting at their ankles with its square nose.

'Sid!' said Patch, grateful for the interruption. She leaned down to scratch him between the ears. 'What are you doing here? Have you lost June?'

'Yoo hoo!' A voice danced on the wind from further along the deck. Forward, thought Patch, remembering Lilian's instructions. Towards the bow end. The call came again, clearer this time. 'Girls! Sid!'

A figure was waving at them. A small figure in a maroon dress trimmed in acid green velvet. A glint of gold.

'It's June Fortune!' said Patch. 'Come on, Sid. Let's take you back.'

But Sid had other ideas. He wouldn't move and he gave short, sharp barks as if he was trying to tell them something. In the end there was nothing to do but pick him up. He weighed a ton – almost as heavy as Patch's carpet bag – but his body was hard and warm and he gave a happy-sounding grunt as she wrapped her arms around him.

'Thank you, girls!' said June when they reached her. 'Naughty Sid. You mustn't go running off.' She reached out to take the dog but he declined the offer, turning his head away to nuzzle under Patch's arm instead.

'Sulking!' said June. 'Because I wouldn't give him any more ginger biscuits! Bring him in, Patch – I can see he's taken a fancy to you. I've got tea and Genoese fancies inside if you want some?' She nodded behind her.

'You're in a regal suite?' Lilian's eyes sparked. 'Mama and Papa stay in one when they travel,' she added quickly.

'Do they, darling?' said June. 'Come and look!'

It *was* a regal suite, fit for kings and queens, with a sitting room, a dining room, two bedrooms and a bathroom. The ceilings were ivory-coloured, all swirly gilding and intricate mouldings, and the walls were papered with a cherry blossom print. Above the fireplace hung a painting of an Italianate villa standing peacefully in a garden with cedar trees. There was a piano and heavy damask curtains and a plush sofa with spindly gold legs.

'In here!' called June and the girls followed her into one of the bedrooms where she retrieved a tray of tea and cakes from a little cupboard in the wall. 'It's called a dumb waiter,' she explained, 'a miniature lift that comes all the way up from the kitchens. Makes life that bit easier for the stewardesses.'

Back in the sitting room, Patch sat at the piano. She had taught herself to play at the uncle's, where she had been expected to take charge of the organ for Sunday service. At the Jenkinses' she had expanded her repertoire at the family singalongs in the church hall on Saturday afternoons.

'Can I?' she asked.

June, pouring tea, nodded yes, and Patch thumped out 'Girl with the Flaxen Hair' for Lilian who looked enraptured as the notes drifted across the cabin. And then surprised as Patch switched tempo and launched into 'Boiled Beef and Carrots' and then 'The Boy I Love is Up in the Gallery' which she sang, as she played, with gusto.

One of the best days of Patch's life had been when

Meg had smuggled her out to the theatre. It had cost sixpence to sit in the balcony, and they'd watched a music hall star called Marie Lloyd. She pretended she was Marie now as she sang.

'The boy I love is up in the gallery,
The boy I love is looking now at me,
There he is, can't you see, waving his handkerchief,
As merry as a robin that sings on a tree.'

'Well I never,' said June, her gold tooth winking. 'I wonder how well that goes down in Mayfair? There's more to you than meets the eye.'

Patch felt like kicking herself. Had she almost blown her cover? Well-to-do girls didn't go around mimicking musical hall stars! She got up and sat next to Lilian on the sofa, hoping June would forget what she had just seen.

The Genoese fancies provided a welcome diversion, delicate little cakes made from crumbly yellow sponge, filled with raspberry jam and butter cream, and iced in pretty pastels. Sid, not to be left out, munched on a ginger biscuit, and June produced a deck of cards and they played snap first, and then, with a different set of cards, happy families. It was warm in the room and the sun slanted through the window, and dust motes danced about in the air.

'Now tell me, darling,' said June to Lilian as she expertly shuffled and then stacked the cards. 'Shouldn't you be in the nursery? Isn't that where unaccompanied children are usually looked after?'

'You mean with the rocking horses and the rattles?' sniffed Lilian dismissively. 'I'm too old for all of that. Anyway, I have Esty.'

'Esty?' echoed June.

'My stewardess. She looks after me.'

'I see,' said June. 'But what will happen when we dock? The stewardess will stay on board presumably and your parents are still in England ...'

'Oh!' said Lilian. For a second she seemed at a loss for words. Patch glanced up. Lilian seemed to be struggling with something. Was it just that she was shy? Except she didn't seem shy. She seemed fairly confident. And she was so clever.

Lilian pushed her spectacles up her nose and in one long breath said, 'There will be a carriage waiting to take me back to the house and Nanny will be there when I arrive, and no doubt there will be meringues and cream for tea.' She looked at them and there was something puzzling in her expression that Patch didn't understand, almost as if she were challenging them to contradict her.

Patch hadn't had meringues and cream for ages. And she was about to say so, when the door to the suite burst open and there stood Mrs Reynolds, resplendent in white lace, a diaphanous scarf wrapped around her creamy throat and, perched on her head, what must have been the biggest picture hat in the world.

'Oh, I do apologise!' she breathed in her whispery voice, a gloved hand flying to her mouth. The white dove on her hat bobbed in agreement. 'I must have got the wrong suite.'

'Are you in a regal one too?' asked Patch.

'Yes, I think so . . .'

'Well, there's another one on the starboard side,' said Lilian.

'Of course! I'm sorry to have interrupted you.'

'How can she not know if she's in a regal suite?' asked Lilian when the unexpected visitor had gone.

'And why doesn't she talk in a normal voice instead of all breathy?' said Patch.

'I could barely hear a thing,' agreed June grabbing a handful of ginger biscuits and scooping Sid up. 'Anyway, it's time for lunch. Would you two care to join us?'

'Not this time thank you, June,' said Patch. She shot

Lilian a look, hoping she had remembered they had made a plan to find Turo.

'Esty is bringing us a picnic,' said Lilian, giving Patch a nod. She *had* remembered.

'So we'll see you at dinner,' added Patch.

Chapter Eight

There was no one operating the lift and so no questions were asked as the girls descended to the main deck.

The lift opened on to a hall with a carpeted corridor on one side and a sturdy-looking iron gate on the other.

'Over the threshold we go,' said Lilian, producing the key from her pocket and, after a furtive glance around, unlocking the gate. 'Welcome to third class.'

The corridor the girls found themselves on was narrower than those in first class. There was no wood panelling on the walls; no plush carpets covering the floor. It was stark and uninviting, just naked lightbulbs dangling from the ceiling and a series of numbered doors. It wasn't fair, thought Patch. Why couldn't everyone enjoy the sumptuous surroundings of the upper decks?

'Where *is* everyone?' she asked. But as soon as the words left her mouth she heard it: first just a murmur, but as they got closer the murmur turned into a babble and the babble became a din, and then a wall of noise.

'They'll be having dinner – I mean lunch – just like upstairs,' said Lilian. She stopped outside a set of double doors. 'See?'

It was a dining hall, jam-packed with people sitting cheek by jowl at long tables stretching from one end of the room to the other. Men, women and children of all ages sat with elbows out, cutlery in hand, talking, eating, scraping plates, laughing. It was warm and fuggy and smelled of Jenkins-type food: boiled beef and onions, mashed potatoes and suet pudding. For a brief moment it filled Patch with longing.

'Lilian? What are you doing down here?'

It was Matty, the copper-haired steward, sitting at the table nearest them and looking extremely surprised to see two first-class girls down in third. Next to him sat Jimmy, the musician. They were both tucking into extremely large bowls of rice pudding with raisins. By their sides lay two musical instruments: a trumpet and a fiddle.

'Matty! We're just exploring – please don't tell Esty!' Lilian pleaded. But Matty wasn't listening. His gaze was fixed on something – or someone – behind the girls.

Standing in the doorway was the weaselly-looking man with the ginger whiskers who Patch had seen yesterday evening. The one who had been staring straight at her when she'd been peeping into the lounge. The new chief steward. The one Lilian had said was to be avoided at all costs.

Patch turned back to Lilian.

But the spot where Lilian had been standing was empty. As if she'd disappeared into thin air.

Something twitched by Patch's foot and glancing down, she saw a boot stealthily disappearing under the table. Was Lilian hiding? Why? What could this weaselly man do to her?

'You're a first-class passenger aren't you?' the chief steward said, stepping towards Patch, his whiskers twitching officiously. 'This really isn't the place for a young lady.'

'You needn't worry' said Patch, thinking quickly. She had seen how her aunt and her grandmother adopted a superior air when it suited them. 'Formidable' was how people described them. Well, she could be formidable herself.

'Jimmy here has invited me to take part in the afternoon concert, isn't that right, Jimmy?' she said, staring hard at the musician, trying to send him an invisible message with her eyes.

'Why sure – on captain's orders,' agreed Jimmy, his eyes twinkling. He pushed his rice pudding aside and grabbed his trumpet. 'What shall we start with? How about a little call and response?'

He put the instrument to his lips and started to play a high, wild, dizzy dancing tune. As the music flooded through her veins, Patch flung back her head and raised her arms, and it was as if the trumpet was calling to her and she was replying. Soon she was spinning and twirling, and all of a sudden she wasn't in a third-class dining room, she was on stage at the Coliseum; and then Matty was picking up his fiddle and the whole room erupted, and everyone was joining in, clapping, stamping, dancing and whirling.

Patch felt alive, lost in the music's magic and she would have danced forever if she hadn't suddenly remembered *why* she was dancing and that Lilian was hiding. Her eyes scanned the room. The chief steward had retreated. Quickly she bent down and pulled at Lilian's foot.

'He's gone!' she hissed.

Lilian scrambled out from underneath the table and dashed from the room, closely followed by Patch, careering along a series of corridors until they came to a spiral staircase leading to the lower deck.

'What was all that about?' gasped Patch as she caught up with her friend.

'I told you we need to avoid him!' said Lilian.

'But why? Because you've got that key?'

Lilian hesitated. 'Yes, and ... Oh, it doesn't matter. Just trust me. He's a troublemaker all right? Esty told me.'

'All right,' said Patch, but Lilian still looked worried.

'He didn't see me, did he?'

'I don't think so,' said Patch. 'You were ever so quick to hide.' She felt there was something that Lilian wasn't telling her. But she wouldn't ask now. They would find Turo first.

As they descended the staircase, a trickle of sweat wended its way down Patch's back. It was getting hotter and hotter the further they went down, and the thrumming sounds of the ship were increasing too.

At the bottom of the staircase was a door marked

'crew only', and then another corridor. Now the flickering lights took on an eerie cast, and the engines rumbled so noisily it felt as if they had stepped deep inside a giant's belly.

'This must be it!' whispered Lilian.

Five or six large-ish rooms led off the corridor, each packed with tiers of bunk beds. The rooms were spartan but meticulously clean. Turo had said how spick and span he kept the crew's quarters. If this was the result of his efforts, he had been telling the truth.

'What's this?' said Patch. They had come to an open hatch, below which lay an almost vertical set of steps.

'Orlop I think,' said Lilian. 'Maybe Turo's down there.'

So Patch descended the steps, which proved to be more of a ladder really – and quite precarious – and Lilian followed. And then just as they reached the bottom, Lilian uttered a sort of strangled cry and Patch froze.

Was that ... a leopard? Teeth glinting, jaw curling, terrible mouth locked into a ferocious snarl?

Leopards lived in the wild or in London Zoo, didn't they? They didn't roam about on ships!

'It's going to kill us!' hissed Lilian.

Or worse, thought Patch, play with them first.

Her limbs felt as though they had turned to ice. She couldn't have moved if she'd wanted to.

And if she *could* move, the leopard would come after her and lock its jaws around her ankles and tug her back down and ...

'Listen!' whispered Lilian.

The ship shuddered. There came more creaking and groaning, like old bones. And then another noise, a sort of knocking, coming from somewhere beyond the leopard. Faint at first, but then getting louder. Patch's brain struggled to make sense of the thing in front of her and what she could hear behind it. Was some poor soul actually lying there, half dead amongst the cargo? Were *they* the leopard's first prey?

She stared at the leopard. The leopard stared back. Its eye was glassy. And the other eye ...

Patch took a step forward.

'Patch,' hissed Lilian. 'Don't!'

'But ...' said Patch. Something wasn't right. The leopard only had one eye.

She reached out and tentatively touched its fur.

Its pelt was smooth and cool ... and totally lifeless. There was no ripple of muscle, no warm blood pumping through its veins.

'It's not real!' Patch exclaimed. Its eye *was* glass, like

a marble. The opposite one was long gone, leaving just an empty socket and a dangling thread.

Round its neck was a label.

DESTINATION:
AMERICAN MUSEUM OF NATURAL HISTORY,
WEST 77TH STREET,
MANHATTAN,
NEW YORK

'And look!'

In the dim light she could pick out more animals, a whole menagerie of them. A lion, a monkey with one arm raised as if in mid-swing, a mean-looking hyena, a black-backed jackal and several parrots that wouldn't have looked out of place on Mrs Reynolds's hat.

The relief made the girls almost hysterical. Patch collapsed onto the floor, her shoulders heaving, stomach aching, and her breath coming in great shuddery gasps. Lilian clambered onto the lion's back, gripping its mane, and pretended to ride it like a horse, which made them both laugh even more.

And then faintly, but just loud enough to cut through their guffaws, came the knocking noise they had heard before.

Abruptly they stopped laughing. The little hairs on Patch's arms prickled. She shivered despite the heat.

'Did you hear that?' asked Lilian sliding off the lion and peering into the gloom. Wherever the knocking was coming from, it seemed to be emanating from deeper inside the hold, lost amongst a looming collection of gigantic crates and boxes.

Patch took a few steps towards the sound. She listened to the sighs and moans of the ship . . . and there it was again! More knocking, almost pounding, getting louder and more frantic. And then, very muffled, a cry.

The girls moved fast now, searching amongst the cargo, bypassing the matching sets of trunks, some covered in alligator skin, others emblazoned with family crests – wardrobe trunks, hat trunks, shoe trunks, dress trunks – scanning the casks and cases, the bales and boxes, the towering crates, a few twice the height of a tall man, all butted together like skyscrapers.

'Help!' Less muffled. More human.

And there, on the floor, was another hatch with 'Ballast, Number Seven, Forward' painted on it in stark white.

'It's coming from down there,' whispered Patch.

'Let's leave it . . .' said Lilian. Her eyes blinked fear behind her spectacles.

'We can't!' said Patch.

There were handles on either side of the wooden cover. Patch took one side and after a moment's hesitation, Lilian took the other. They heaved and—

Lilian screamed again.

Below the hatch, a disembodied head was resting on top of mounds and mounds of what looked like gravel or sand. The head moved a bit. Two wild eyes swivelled in their direction. The thing's mouth opened.

'What is it? What is it?' screamed Lilian, backing away.

Patch stayed where she was. The thing was *stuck* in the sandy gravel. Drowned, almost. It couldn't hurt them while it was trapped like that.

Its mouth opened and it gasped, its hands protruding from the sand. An empty bottle lay to one side.

'It's trying to say something,' said Patch, fascinated.

'About time!' it managed hoarsely.

Another gasp and then the thing shook its head like a dog coming out of water, releasing the gravelly sand that clung to its hair and face so that it sprayed out in all directions, catching them and stinging their skin.

'Please,' it croaked. A woman's voice. 'For pity's sake, dig me out!'

Chapter Nine

They leaned over the hatch and dug and dug, thrusting their hands deep into the gravel, scooping it up and chucking it to one side until it made a small mountain. They helped the woman out and watched as she feebly brushed the layers of sandy dust from her hair and her clothes, and from the giant bag that she lugged out after her.

Patch and Lilian exchanged shocked stares. Patch had never come across anything so remarkable. What on earth had the woman been *doing* down there?

'Must...Lie...Down...' the woman rasped, gently lowering herself to the floor. A pair of bright red satin shoes peeped out from underneath her indigo-coloured skirt. A cloud of wild black hair tumbled in a tangled mess down her back. There was something piratical about her.

'Been in there too long. When did we set sail?' she asked, her voice still feeble.

'Yesterday,' said Lilian.

There was a short silence while the woman appeared to be totting up the days in her head.

'Since . . . Friday, so that's . . .'

'Five days,' offered Patch.

The woman nodded and tried to sit up, but on second thoughts lay down again. 'I'm usually strong as an ox. Not strong enough to dig my own way out of two hundred tonnes of ballast, though,' she said, with a wry laugh. 'Lord knows why I didn't stick to my usual methods.'

'Did someone *put* you down there?' asked Patch. She could imagine nothing more dreadful than being buried alive. A fate worse than death.

'Oh darling, no!' said the woman. 'I was hiding!'

The woman was a stowaway! A real one.

'Thank *goodness* you girls came along and saved my bacon. I'm Babette, by the way.'

'I'm Patch,' said Patch, 'and this is Lilian.'

'Patch, could you be a dear and pass me my mirror? It's in the bag.'

Patch opened the bag. It was large, even larger than her own carpet bag, and it was stuffed full. There looked to be all kinds of treasures in there: a short brown wig, a pair of spectacles, a shimmering evening dress.

The mirror, small and silver-backed, was in a side compartment. Patch passed it to Babette, who, on examining her reflection from her prone position gave a little wail.

'No wonder I scared you both out of your wits!'

'Did you have anything to eat when you were buried?' asked Patch. Babette looked ever so pale.

'I had a piece of German sausage that lasted for three-and-a-half days,' said Babette, 'and I finished my water yester . . .'

With a sigh she shut her eyes. It was clearly too much of an effort to speak.

'I think she's going to faint!' said Lilian. She grabbed the empty water bottle and disappeared into the warren of trunks and suitcases. A few minutes later, she reappeared, the water bottle filled to the brim. She sprinkled a bit on Babette's forehead.

Babette's lips were very dry – a sort of bluey-white colour instead of pink. Patch rummaged in the bag and found a woollen scarf. She folded it into a sort of pillow and rested it under Babette's head.

'She needs sustenance,' Patch said to Lilian. 'D'you think there's any food hanging about in the crew's quarters?'

'I doubt it ... but the storerooms are on the lower deck,' said Lilian. 'I've not been inside them, but I've seen them. They must be full of stuff.'

'Quick then!' said Patch. 'I'm fast, I'll go, but you'd better stay here, make sure she's all right. Will I need the key?'

Lilian took the master key out of her pocket and passed it to Patch. 'They're aft – at the other end of the ship. Just keep going past the boiler rooms and the bunkers. The doors are all labelled, you can't miss them. Bring back as much as you can carry.'

* * *

The noise at the other end of the ship was monstrous – great tremblings, and close by, other sounds on top of the usual vibrations: rumbles and clangs and unearthly shouts. Patch, usually so brave, was relieved when she reached the storerooms. They were all labelled, just as Lilian had said they would be: Mutton and Poultry, Beef, Bacon, Flour, Potatoes, Fruit and Vegetables, Groceries.

It was eerie down here all on her own. She couldn't wait to grab the supplies and get back to Lilian. But just as she was lifting the key to the lock, something made her pause. What was that? Was someone coming? Bother! What if it was the chief steward? Always sticking his nose into other people's business, Lilian had said. He was bound to stop her and question her, and then she wouldn't be able to get the provisions back to Babette in time. And then what would happen? Would Babette die? She had looked very weak.

Furiously, Patch jammed the key in the lock and tried to turn it. If she could just get into the storeroom she could hide.

But the key wouldn't turn – it seemed to have stuck, so she yanked it out. The footsteps were closer now.

Patch's gaze swivelled up and down the corridor. There was an oval-shaped metal door in the wall a little further along. Would that be open? Perhaps she could conceal herself behind it just for a few minutes, until whoever it was had passed. She skittered across to it and using all her strength, she hefted it open and stepped inside. The door clanged noisily shut behind her and a great blast of heat hit her squarely in the face. She was at the top of a steep iron ladder. And at the bottom . . .

It was like another world. A world that looked like hell: black and fiery and piercingly hot and loud.

There were actually men down there, lots of them, some in caps and overalls, others stripped to the waist. Patch stared, transfixed. Back and forth they went, their bodies streaked with sweat and coal dust, shovelling coal from bunkers into barrows, carting it across to more men, who hurled it into the mouths of roaring furnaces.

Behind her, the door rattled. The chief steward *had* seen her! And he was trying to get in. What should she do? She couldn't go further down. Not to . . . *that*. But she couldn't go back either.

The engines boomed and a gong crashed, and then the men by the furnaces stepped away and a new gang emerged from the shadows, and the furious business of shovelling and carting and hurling began all over again.

The door behind Patch burst open, a hand shot in, grabbed her and pulled her back out into the passageway.

'What are you doing? Do you wanna get hurt?'

It wasn't the chief steward, it was a boy in a jersey with Cunard stitched across it.

'Turo!' she said. She was half angry at being discovered. Half relieved to be rescued from what she had just witnessed.

'Patch?' He blinked furiously as if he couldn't quite believe what he was seeing. 'Whaddaya doin' here? And why d'you go in the boiler room?'

'Never mind about that,' she exclaimed. 'Do you realise you got me into the most terrible trouble? After you stole that toffee, they called the constable! I had to skate like the clappers and I followed you onto the ship, but you'd done a vanishing act and then I had to hide and the ship set sail!'

'Whoah!' he said.

'And I never even *gave* you my roller skate,' she said. 'Some people would say you *stole* it.'

Turo had the grace to look sheepish. 'Sorry. I'll give it you back. But . . .' He looked back at the metal door. 'What *were* you doin' in there?'

'I came to get supplies for . . .' she broke off. How was she to know if Turo could be trusted? 'I heard footsteps. Thought you were the chief steward.'

'Perkins? You're right to avoid him,' said Turo. He looked over his shoulder. 'Captain prides himself on having a stowaway-free ship – offers a pint of grog to anyone who catches one. An' I've heard Perkins boasting about how good he is at seeking them out.'

'Would you turn *me* in?' asked Patch. 'For grog?'

Turo burst out laughing and straight away Patch

remembered how much she had liked him. How he hadn't taken offence when she'd been cross, how he seemed to accept her despite her prickliness. 'Are you crazy?' he continued cheerfully. 'I hate grog. Anyway, it's my fault you're here so it would hardly be fair to turn you in.'

'Look,' said Patch, thinking about Babette and Lilian waiting for her. 'I haven't got long. Will you help me carry some stuff back to the cargo hold?'

'That where you hidin'?' asked Turo, and Patch gave a sort of imperceptible nod because she hadn't yet quite worked out how much she could tell him.

'Well sure, I can help ya,' said Turo. 'I'm going back that way. Just came to get some more soap for crew's quarters.'

This time the key turned perfectly. In Groceries, Patch grabbed several tins of dry biscuits and cheese. In Fruit and Vegetables she found oranges. Turo produced a jug and filled it with water and chips of ice.

Back out on the corridor, they were just about to set off when a shrill bell rang out. A look of concern flitted across Turo's features.

'Holy moly. Stand back,' he urged. 'Until—'

His words were lost in a burst of clattering, and just as Patch had pressed herself flat against the passage wall, the metal door clanged open and a throng of the men she had seen working below clambered out, covered in soot and smelling of sweat and heat and singed hair. They stamped past, shouting in loud gruff voices just like the dustcart men in Lambeth. A frightening sort of shouting, the sort which seems to be halfway between fighting and laughing.

And then, almost as quickly as they had come, they had gone.

'Wait!' said Turo as Patch started to move off.

There was still someone down there. A scrabbling noise, the rasp of laboured breathing, a guttural cough. And then another stoker man lurched out, took several unsteady steps towards them, and collapsed like a rag doll at their feet.

He looked half dead, Patch thought.

She peered back along the passage, the way the other stokers had gone, but they had disappeared. She looked back at the man. His eyes were fixed on hers, bright and wild in his soot-covered face.

'Please . . .' he gasped. His hand reached for her foot. For one terrible moment she thought he was going to grab her ankle and pull her back towards that metal door and to the horrors that lay below.

'No!' she said, stepping back and colliding with Turo.

'Please . . . water . . .' The man's voice was hoarse. He took a long, rattly breath. The effort of speaking took its toll and his head thudded to the floor.

'Have you got a cup?' asked Turo. He had picked the jug up and was looking about for something to pour it into.

'No,' said Patch. 'But this will do.' Quickly she unlaced her boot, tugged it off and gestured at Turo to fill it up. It made a cup of sorts.

They both crouched down and Turo gently lifted the man's head while Patch tipped up the boot and held it to his lips. He swallowed pitifully.

A bead of sweat trickled its way down Patch's forehead. The boilers below rumbled on, belching out heat. She dipped a corner of her dress into the cool water and squeezed it onto the man's forehead.

'What's your name?' she asked.

'Scully,' the man whispered.

'Here, Scully.' She peeled one of the oranges, tore it into segments, scraped away the pith with her fingernail and pressed a piece into his hand. The juice dribbled down his chin but he chewed hungrily and asked for more, and then more water. Gradually, his breathing lengthened and the rasps became less.

'I gorra ge' back to me bunk now. Can you . . .'

He reached for something round his neck, pulled it over his head and held it out shakily to Patch. It was a small silver whistle. Or it would have been silver once upon a time if it hadn't been so smothered in coal dust.

'Twice should do it,' he said. He still sounded very weak. 'And they'll come.'

Patch held the whistle to her lips and blew two short sharp whistles.

Painfully slowly, the man got to his feet and then, with Patch holding him up on one side and Turo on the other, they began to inch their way along the passage. They had only gone a few yards when there was a clatter and stamp and several of the fearsome-looking men reappeared, their eyes glinting in their dusty faces.

'Scully! You whistled! You all right?'

Patch couldn't understand half of what they were saying, but she thought she detected words like 'kind chil'un' and 'thank-ye' floating through their rough Liverpudlian twang. And then they were hoisting Scully up – 'heave-ho!' – and moving off down the passage.

'Wait!' Patch called. She was still holding the whistle.

The men stopped and Scully looked back over his shoulder.

'You keep it,' he croaked. 'And if you ever need owt, just blow twice. We'll come.'

'Thank you,' said Patch faintly, and then they were gone.

Chapter Ten

Turo and Patch walked back together. When they got to the hatch Patch was adamant that Turo needn't come down. She pretended that it was *her* hiding place. She would take the food down first and come back for the water. He looked at her oddly, but agreed.

'At last!' said Lilian when Patch appeared with the supplies. Lilian had dug out a fur coat from Babette's capacious carpet bag and covered her with it, as if it were a blanket. Even so, she was still shivering despite the boiling heat.

Babette took a biscuit eagerly, and then a piece of cheese. She had just taken a first bite when they heard a thud followed by the patter of feet.

'Patch!' a hoarse whisper. 'I got your roller skate.'

A head popped round one of the giant crates. Turo. His gaze took in Patch and Lilian, but it was when it landed on Babette that he did a double take.

'What's he doing here?' hissed Lilian. 'Did he follow you?'

But Patch didn't reply. She was watching the way Turo was staring at Babette. A look of admiration. Of awe. Did he know something they didn't?

His eyes whipped from the mound of ballast to Babette's giant bag and back to Babette again.

'It's you!' he said.

His voice was full of wonder. His eyes round as saucers.

Babette smiled. She nodded graciously, like a Queen bestowing greetings on one of her subjects.

'It *is*, isn't it!' he said. 'I've collected all your postcards!'

'What postcards?' asked Patch. Lilian was looking equally befuddled. 'What're you talking about?'

Babette raised herself onto her elbows. 'At last! Someone who knows who I am!'

'What do you mean, who you are?' said Patch.

'Are you famous?' asked Lilian.

'You bet she is,' said Turo. He had taken off his cap

and gave Babette a little bow. 'You're only looking at the World's Greatest Stowaway!'

'I am rather well known,' agreed Babette, 'in the world of ocean liners.'

Turo's words seemed to have a positive effect on her. She pulled herself up and then shuffled along so she was able to recline against a nearby crate. Taking the water bottle from Lilian, she took a good long slug and then crammed a large chunk of cheese into her mouth, followed by a bite of biscuit.

'Do you mean to say you've done this before?' asked Patch.

'Why, yes, dear child, I'm not an amateur.' Babette wasn't bothered about speaking with her mouth full. It seemed that now she had started on the cheese and biscuits she couldn't stop, barely swallowing each mouthful before taking another bite. 'But I've never hidden in ballast before. And I never will again. I usually take shelter in a lifeboat, but I've also hidden in an empty flour barrel, I've dressed as a labourer, and I've concealed myself in coal bunkers, although that method can be a bit risky.' An elegant hand reached up to push back her huge cloud of hair. Her eyes were alight. 'I've seen the world, my darlings! Buenos Aires, Cape Town, Zanzibar . . . I've even waltzed onto a ship in broad daylight. It's all about knowing the right time.'

'The right time?' echoed Patch, thinking that was exactly what she'd done, waltzed onto this very ship in broad daylight. And she hadn't been caught either, even if she was what Babette would call an amateur!

Unless ... She shook the thought of Mr Reynolds and his horrible sapphire-coloured eyes away.

'Five days before a ship sets sail is best,' said Babette. 'There's always such a great deal of confusion going on. All the comings and goings, the changes of crew, the stokers, the cooks, the stewards. You wouldn't believe how easy it is for the officers to think that a strange face belongs to a new hand!'

'And you've never been caught!' said Turo.

'Never! I'm the best!'

The grandmother would have told Babette to be a little more modest. The aunt would have said not to boast. Patch didn't agree. If you were really good at something, what was the harm in saying so?

'But ...we caught you,' said Lilian shyly.

'Darlings! You didn't catch me, you *rescued* me. A stowaway survives on the kindness of strangers. We make friends. We trust our judgement. That's how we manage. That and our disguises.' She smiled at Patch, her eyes twinkling charmingly.

Patch couldn't help thinking how *she* had good judgement too. She'd known to make friends with Lilian and now Turo. They would help *her* manage.

'But what about your home?' she asked. Babette's boldness intrigued her. 'Do you have one? Or are you always at sea?'

'Always at sea,' said Babette. 'The thing is, I have the most *terrible* land legs. They go quite wobbly the minute they make contact with solid earth! It *would* be nice to have a home ...' For a minute she looked wistful. 'But I can't! I itch if I'm not moving. I can't stay still. If I'm made to stay in one place for too long it feels like torture. When we dock in New York you won't see me for dust. I'll be straight onto another ship. Ahoy me hearties! Here I come.'

They all stared at Babette, absorbing this rather astonishing information.

'If it's so much easier hiding in lifeboats then why *did* you bury yourself in the ballast?' asked Patch, thinking about the empty water bottle and the German sausage which had only lasted for a few days. It seemed like madness. 'What if we hadn't come?'

'Because the World's Greatest Stowaway has to live up to her name,' said Babette. 'Take risks, be brave, be brazen. And anyway, you *did* come, so what's the worry? Pass my bag would you?'

Lilian pushed the bag towards Babette and they watched while she delved inside and pulled out a small notebook.

'We left Liverpool yesterday, yes?' she asked, rifling through the pages. From behind her ear she took a pencil, rubbed it against her skirt and began to scribble intently. '*Everything* is in here. All the places I've been to and all the places I'm going to. Would you like a postcard? They normally sell for a penny each, but seeing as you helped a friend in need ...'

The postcards were printed with pictures of all the ports that Babette had ever sailed into, and superimposed on top of these was a photograph of Babette herself. The photograph was a bit fuzzy but you could still see it was her. She wore a canary yellow dress and the same red shoes that she had on now. In swirly print at the bottom were the words, 'Bonjour from Babette,' and below that, 'The World's Greatest Stowaway!'

'Are you French?' asked Patch. She had learned a little of the language from one of the governesses at the aunt's house.

'My great-grandmamma taught me a love for all things French, and I do like the way "*bonjour*" sounds next to my name!' said Babette. 'Would you like to see my disguises?'

'Oh, yes please,' said Turo.

'Well,' said Babette, 'when I'm on board, I have three changes of costume.'

'So you can flit about between first, second and third class!' guessed Turo.

'Yes,' said Babette. 'The first rule of a good stowaway – always wear the correct attire. Look, this is my first-class outfit.' She drew out an oyster-coloured satin-and-lace dress with a flourish. It certainly wouldn't have looked out of place in the grand dining saloon.

'This is second class,' she continued, shaking out a sober-looking green plaid dress, 'and this ragbag lot' – she held up a dark skirt and a moth-eaten woollen shawl – 'are for when I'm in third.'

'And what about all the other stuff,' asked Patch, 'the wig and whatnot?'

'Oh, I have a whole box of tricks,' Babette said. 'Wigs, spectacles, moustaches, toupees – I can pass for a man if necessary.' She lowered her voice by a gruff octave. 'Anything to help get me out of a fix.'

They all burst out laughing. Babette was good. Really good. Patch could learn a lot from her. Perhaps she should tell her she was a stowaway too?

But all of a sudden Babette stopped talking and lay down again. It was as if all the wind had gone out of her sails. She gave a little shudder and sighed. 'This is most unlike me. I'll manage with the biscuits and cheese today. But do you know what, I'd really like a pint of beef tea.'

'We'll bring some tomorrow,' said Patch quickly.

'If you could, darling,' said Babette, 'that would be divine.'

* * *

Lilian didn't want to go to the dining saloon that night.

'It's too dangerous,' she said.

Patch didn't understand. She thought she'd been performing the part of Patchouli Cooper-Gordon perfectly. She was enjoying hiding in plain sight. Mr Reynolds hadn't said anything. He mustn't have put two and two together. Jimmy and June believed in her. Why couldn't they just carry on as they had been?

But Lilian didn't agree.

'You don't understand about the chief steward,' she said. 'Always sneaking about, poking his nose into other people's business. He's noticed you now, with all that dancing. You've got to be more careful.'

So Patch hid in the WC while Esty brought Lilian's supper on a tray. And after Esty had gone they shared cold roast chicken followed by treacle tart.

'Did you ask her to get you some beef tea for tomorrow?' Patch asked, thinking about Babette all weak and wan in the hold.

'I forgot,' admitted Lilian.

'Lilian!' said Patch. 'We promised we'd—'

'I'll ask in the morning,' interjected Lilian. 'Listen! I reckon it'll be safe to go up on deck for a bit. It'll be dark and you can teach me how to roller skate.'

She was changing the subject, thought Patch. For some reason Lilian was reluctant to ask for the beef tea. Well, tomorrow *she* would work out a way to get the beef tea for Babette. She felt an allegiance towards her because they were both stowaways, even if Babette didn't know it yet.

* * *

To get to the boat deck, they had to walk past the dining saloon.

'See?! He's there!' said Lilian. And sure enough, Patch could see the chief steward parading around the perimeter of the saloon in an extremely officious manner. She could see their table too. Tonight, Jimmy wasn't in his usual place because he was fronting the band. Sid was under the table with a plate of ginger biscuits. Mr Reynolds was demolishing a platter of oysters. June and Mrs Reynolds looked deep in conversation.

Up on the boat deck, the whole ship was lit up, glints of gold dancing across the black sea. They buckled up a skate each and then Patch held Lilian's hand and showed her how to push off with one foot, once, twice, three times and then sail along before pushing off again. Lilian was a quick learner and Patch was just about to teach her how to zigzag when they heard a door slam further up the deck.

'What if it's . . .' Lilian said. Her face was white in the moonlight. She looked genuinely scared.

'C'mon!' Patch darted into the shadows of one of the giant funnels and Lilian followed. No one would see them here.

A whiff of cologne and tobacco. The tap of a stick on the wooden floor. A large hat crammed with feathers and flowers.

'It's Mr and Mrs Reynolds,' whispered Patch.

'It's always a game with you isn't it?' they heard Mr Reynolds say as the couple drew close. 'By dressing up in fancy clothes, you think you can get up to whatever you please!'

A sudden gust of wind whipped up, drowning out Mrs Reynolds's reply. By the time the wind had dropped, Mr Reynolds was speaking again.

'I thought we agreed – once on board you'd stay out of sight . . . Only for five days . . . Three helpings of beef and oyster pie! Have you gone crackers?'

Patch listened, feeling more and more indignant. She had suspected there was something of the child-hater about Mr Reynolds. She'd seen it in his eyes, which were like cold, hard marbles. But here was proof that he was a woman-hater too. Poor Mrs Reynolds! No wonder she was so quiet and whispery.

Without thinking, she burst out from behind the funnel.

'Ignore him!' she said to Mrs Reynolds. 'Women are allowed out in society just the same as men! And if you want three helpings of pie, he mustn't stop you!'

'Patch!' Lilian was tugging at her elbow. Mr and Mrs Reynolds stopped dead in their tracks. They stared at Patch with a mixture of surprise and horror. Mr Reynolds raised one eyebrow so high it seemed to disappear into his grey-black curls. Mrs Reynolds's white-gloved hand rushed to her throat.

'Well, well, if it isn't our little heiress and ... friend.' Mr Reynolds waved his cigar at them and took a long puff, the tip glowing orange in the dark. Mrs Reynolds clutched her fur and shivered.

'And how is Miss de Haviland? We missed you at dinner today.' He smiled at Lilian, slightly wolfishly Patch thought. 'Looking forward to getting home are you?' He gave a slight bow.

'Oh yes,' replied Lilian. 'I can't wait to see Fifth Avenue again!'

'Good, good,' said Mr Reynolds. He tapped his cane twice on the ground and then swung it up so that it rested on his shoulder the way the marching guards at Buckingham Palace held their rifles. 'Well, it's very late – time to turn in, dear?'

'Yes, darling,' said Mrs Reynolds in her whispery voice. 'Goodnight, children.'

'Goodnight,' they replied.

'Lilian,' Patch said after they had gone. 'Why did he call you an heiress?'

'Because I might have mentioned to June at dinner yesterday that my father is one of the richest men in Manhattan,' said Lilian, fiddling with her spectacles. 'He must've heard.'

'I don't like him,' said Patch. 'You heard the way he

was talking to Mrs Reynolds. Why were you so polite? He's horrid.'

'Because,' said Lilian, 'you don't seem to realise that if you're to stay under cover, you've got to blend in. Not make a fuss, nor cause a scene. Can you do that?'

'I suppose so,' said Patch a bit mutinously. But the truth was, she didn't know if she *could* do what Lilian was asking. If something was wrong she would challenge it.

And there *was* something wrong about Mr Reynolds. She just didn't know what yet.

Chapter Eleven

When Patch woke the next day, the familiar thrum of the ship was mixed with something different. The constant vibration was still there, but this new thing came and went, a sort of rolling swell that made your tummy flip up and somersault over.

Patch lay still, her body adapting to the new sensation. From the other bed came a long, low groan.

Patch sat up and peered at her friend. 'Lilian. Are you all right?'

She wasn't all right. She was sickly pale, a sort of ghostly green.

'Didn't I tell you,' she said, her eyes burning black, her face all tight, 'it's not always blue skies and calm sailing … Oh … Patch, I'm going to be sick – quick, under the bed, get the bucket!'

Patch jumped out of bed and immediately fell over. It felt like the world beneath her was disappearing, the floor running away so fast she couldn't stand up. She gripped the side of the bed and waited for the rolling to subside.

'Patch, the bucket!' Lilian groaned again, more urgently.

This time Patch did manage to stand despite the fact that the room was still tilting at an alarming angle. Tentatively she took a step towards her friend. The boat tilted once more, she staggered awkwardly and reeled backwards.

Perhaps the thing to do was try and move in time with the swell, ride with it, rather than fight it. The room tipped again and for a split second she was on the verge of toppling, but then she imagined there were magnets stuck to the soles of her feet and she stayed upright.

'Patch,' moaned Lilian.

Patch managed to cross the room and drag the steel bucket out from under the bed. Just in time she shoved it at Lilian, who heaved into it, damp strands of hair plastered to her forehead, features pallid with a sweaty sheen. 'Why can't there be just one calm crossing?' she said, flopping back onto her pillow when she was done.

'Let me get you some water,' said Patch, tottering back across the room to fetch a cup. The porthole was a mass of stormy greys. She pressed her face up close but she could barely see a thing, just rain and seawater lashing angrily against the glass.

The boat lurched and she remembered a painting she'd once seen at the National Gallery, of a ship being tossed and turned on waves the size of skyscrapers. Don't think about it, Patch, she told herself and concentrated instead on holding the cup to Lilian's lips.

Gently she smoothed back her friend's hair, the way Meg once had when she'd been sick herself. Lilian's skin was cold and clammy.

'You'll feel better in a minute,' she said hopefully.

'I won't,' moaned Lilian. 'I'll feel dreadful all day. I get rotten seasickness and it takes ages and ages to get over it, even after the storm has ended. Oh, do give me the bucket again!'

Patch watched helplessly. What was it Turo had said about guarding against seasickness? That passengers should lie down in the middle of the boat, not eat anything for two days and then drink iced champagne?

Surely he didn't mean to do that in these conditions? Patch chanced a look out of the porthole again. In her mind's eye she pictured the deck half drowned in rain, the promenade slick with seawater.

Lilian's teeth chattered. She was hardly in a fit state to be marched up on deck, let alone get out of bed.

'Lilian.'

Patch jerked round. The cabin door had opened and there was Esty holding a tray of tea and toast in one hand, a bucket of water and towels in the other. The ship pitched once more and water spilled over the sides of the bucket, trickling into the cabin and lapping at Patch's feet.

'Patchouli!' Esty said, sliding the tray onto the bedside table and simultaneously dropping the towels. The boat swayed and she clutched on to the doorframe. 'What are you doing here? It's a bit early!'

Patch glanced at Lilian to see if she would come to her rescue, but Lilian was beyond smoothing things over. Patch would just have to manage on her own.

'Let me help,' she said, springing forward to pick up the towels and arrange them on the bed in an attempt to disguise the crumpled sheets. 'Lilian told me she gets seasick, so I came to see if she was all right ...' she trailed off.

'That's kind of you ...' Esty dipped a facecloth into the bucket of water, wrung it out and passed it to Patch. 'Would you mind holding that to her forehead – just like that, yes, good – while I go and wash this out.'

Esty disappeared, taking the sick bucket with her. Quickly Patch straightened the quilt on her bed, rearranged the towels, and then pressed the cool cloth against Lilian's skin. The cabin tipped to and fro. Lilian whimpered. The pile of books that stood on the desk slid from one side to the other and crashed to the floor. Lilian winced and squeezed her eyes tight shut.

The door opened and Esty was back. 'How is she now?'

'Poorly,' said Patch. Lilian heaved again. 'I think she needs beef tea.'

'Not Lilian,' said Esty with the glimmer of a smile. 'She can't stand the stuff, can you dear?'

'Couldn't eat a thing,' said Lilian.

Patch bent down to smooth Lilian's pillow and nudged her surreptitiously with her elbow. 'Beef tea will make you stronger,' she said meaningfully.

'Maybe I should try some,' said Lilian feebly.

'Well, that's a turn up for the books,' said Esty. 'But I can't get it now – I've got a million things to do. All my other ladies will be calling for me ...'

'I can get it,' chipped in Patch. 'If you tell me where to go.'

'Your parents wouldn't be too happy about me sending you along to the kitchen. But . . .' Esty pushed a strand of hair behind her ears, glanced worriedly at Lilian, her forehead puckered in a frown.

'I won't tell them,' said Patch quickly. 'Please let me go.'

'Very well then,' agreed Esty, and a shadow of something – was it relief? – passed over her features.

'The door to the kitchen is at the rear of the dining saloon. Ask for Mrs Chilkes. Say I sent you.'

In the corridor the lurches came thick and fast, each one more violent than the last. It was hard to walk in a straight line so Patch had to zigzag from one side of the corridor to the other, arms outstretched. From behind the closed doors of the other cabins came the sound of distant moans. Poor Lilian wasn't the only person suffering then.

The dining saloon, when Patch came to it, was gloomily deserted, with only a fraction of grey light filtering through the huge glass dome. The whole room swayed to and fro as if it were drunk. Patch had seen a drunk man once on the London Underground. He'd wobbled about scarily but Meg had said if he bothered them, they'd only have to tap him once and he'd fall over.

Now Patch moved cautiously from table to table, managing to stay upright until at last she reached the door at the back. She paused, listening to the sounds of shouting and the crash of crockery on the other side. Should she knock? Or just go straight in? But then the ship jerked and the door slammed open, and she almost fell through on a wave of smashes and shrieks. A fork came flying through the air, hurtling straight for her. She ducked just in time and it missed her ear by an inch.

'Watch it!' an imposing-looking woman shouted, holding three chickens in one hand and trying to catch a glass bowl that was sliding towards the edge of the counter with another. 'Don't just stand there. Pick those up!' She indicated a sea of cutlery on the floor, clinking about at Patch's feet.

'I'm just here to—' started Patch, but the woman frowned and shouted, 'Not now!' in the sort of voice that there is no arguing with, and so Patch bent down and started to pick up the knives and forks and spoons, looking up just in time to grab the tray the woman tossed at her. 'In there, and make it quick before we roll again.'

The cutlery clattered noisily as Patch scooped it up

and tossed it into the tray, not bothering about sorting it out into the correct compartments.

'Gerr'out of the way!' barked a figure dressed in whites, shoving Patch aside to give a pot of something a brisk stir. The ship dipped, someone shouted, 'Steady as she goes,' and Patch bashed into another cook in an effort to avoid the sloshes of boiling liquid erupting from one of the giant pans.

'There you are!' It was the imposing-looking woman again. 'Hold this.' She thrust a steaming pan at Patch. Patch took it, the ship gave another violent lurch, and a volley of hot potatoes tumbled out, scalding her hand.

'Ouch!' she cried, letting go of the pan, and then watching in horror as the pan shot upwards, turned over in mid-air and then crashed to the floor with a thud.

It would have been funny if it wasn't so awful.

'Who in thunder *are* you?' said the woman.

'I'm looking for Mrs Chilkes,' said Patch, backing away. 'I did try to tell you.'

'You're talking to her,' the woman said. 'What do you want me for? It'd better be good.'

'Esty sent me,' Patch wavered. The woman was quite a bit more frightening than any drunk man.

But miraculously, the name seemed to work like

a sort of calming balm and Mrs Chilkes' fierceness evaporated. Nodding in the direction of a smaller room leading off the kitchen, she said, 'In there.'

'In there' was the pantry, several degrees cooler than the kitchen and with an air of order to it that in other circumstances would have been soothing. Patch's eyes roved over the shelves neatly lined with all sorts of recognisable things: salt, spices, custard powder, tapioca.

'Well?' said Mrs Chilkes, looming in the door.

'I've been sent for beef tea. We need it for Lilian. Esty looks after her.'

'Well lawks' sake, why didn't you say that straight away? Look in that cupboard will you, and you'll find a bowl of beef steeping in water. Drain it and heat it through and it's yours.'

Mrs Chilkes' looked at Patch properly for the first time. Her eyes took in the old-fashioned sailor dress and smart black leather boots and she suddenly looked doubtful. 'Parents know you're here, do they? Are you capable?'

'Yes,' said Patch, ignoring the first question but answering the second because it was true. She *was* capable. When she'd been in Lambeth she had watched Mrs Jenkins roast a precious joint of mutton on a

Sunday and serve just a fraction of it, eking it out for the rest of the week – in thin stews, thick broths and finally in watery gravy to flavour meagre plates of cabbage and potato.

So Patch collected the beef. She found a piece of muslin and drained the liquid through the muslin and set the beef aside. She braved the cacophony of the kitchen again to grab a small saucepan from the overhead rack. She took it into the pantry and poured the beef water into it. Then she took the pan back into the kitchen and set it on one of the stoves, stirring it with a wooden spoon while it heated through.

'Well, wonders will never cease,' said Mrs Chilkes, appearing from the pantry. 'Now pour it in here.' She offered Patch a heavy, cream-coloured jug and watched while Patch filled it to the brim with the tea.

'Just you remember. I'm always here for Esty and her girl, grog or no grog.'

'Pardon?' Wasn't grog what the captain gave as a reward in exchange for handing over stowaways? That's what Turo had said. Did that mean Mrs Chilkes had somehow guessed that *she* was a stowaway? The ship lurched sickeningly.

'Never you mind,' said Mrs Chilkes. 'Subject closed. Now off you go and watch none of that spills.'

Chapter Twelve

When Patch arrived back at the cabin, Lilian was still as pale as death but she was sitting up in bed reading.

'What's that?' asked Patch. It looked like a school exercise book.

'Nothing important,' said Lilian, putting the book under the covers.

Patch was about to whip the covers back to take a closer look, but there was something in Lilian's expression that stopped her. Anyway, she didn't want to get into an argument now. She wanted to give Lilian her share of the beef tea and then take the rest down to Babette. She'd be so pleased when she saw her request had been met.

'Come on then, time for your beef tea.'

'Ugh, no!' said Lilian. 'I wouldn't drink it if you paid me one hundred pounds. I can't bear the stuff. I'll be sick all over again if you make me.'

'Well then, I'm going to take it down to Babette,' said Patch. '*She'll* be grateful, at least.'

'Oh do, Patch,' said Lilian, and lying back down with a dreadfully long sigh to rival one of Mr Ringe's, she closed her eyes.

* * *

The first thing Patch saw as she approached the crew's quarters was Turo. He had his sleeves rolled up, his elbows deep in a bucket of soap suds, and he was lost in concentration as he scrubbed the floor.

'Turo!' she said, rushing towards him, and then stopping to cover the top of the beef tea jug with her hands as the ship gave another roll. 'Guess what I've got!'

But instead of looking as pleased to see her as she was him, he put his finger to his lips and waggled his eyebrows.

'What are you making that funny face for?'

'Sshhh!' his eyes flitted further along the corridor and back to Patch again. 'The new chief steward is doing his inspections! If he catches you down here it'll be . . .' He mimed slitting his throat.

'Boy! What's going on?'

Patch jumped and took a step backwards but it was too late. The chief steward was marching straight towards them. Her heart sank. He seemed to be everywhere, popping up all over the place like a jack-in-the-box!

'What have we here then? Highly irregular to see a young miss below the waterline! Didn't I see you yesterday in the third-class dining room?'

'I don't know,' said Patch, playing for time.

The boat shifted and a splosh of beef tea leapt over the rim of the jug.

'What's that you've got there?'

'Beef tea. For Lilian. Mrs Chilkes gave it to me.'

The man's flinty eyes widened a fraction. 'She did, did she?'

'Yes,' said Patch defensively.

'Well which deck is this Louise on?'

'Lilian, not Louise,' said Patch impatiently. She wished he would go away, stop interfering, so that she could go down into the hold and see Babette. Honestly, she didn't see why he had to meddle in other people's business. Didn't he have anything better to do?

'Just answer the question,' said Perkins.

'Oh, for goodness sake! Upper deck, if you must know,' said Patch without thinking.

'Well now, that *is* curious,' said Perkins, and he twiddled his ginger whiskers with a self-satisfied air. 'Last time I looked, Mrs Chilkes' kitchen was on the upper deck too. So . . . tell me again, how did you end up down here? Let me see . . .' He made a show of counting on his fingers. 'That's . . . three decks below?'

Inwardly Patch cursed herself. He was trying to trap her. She hadn't been quick enough. 'I've got a terrible sense of direction,' she blustered.

'I'll say you have.' Chief Steward Perkins smirked.

'Shall I show her back up, sir?' cut in Turo. He had wrung every last drop of water out of the floor cloth and was twisting it back and forth in his hands.

'No,' said Perkins. 'You shan't.'

He was standing right by the ladder that led down to the hold. Now he looked from Patch to the ladder and back again. His gaze hardened.

'A little bird tells me it's not beyond the bounds of possibility that you intended to take that tea down into the hold . . .'

'A little bird told you no such thing!' retorted Patch before she could stop herself. She knew she should stay calm, not take the bait. But there was something about this man that made that line of action singularly impossible. 'You're just making things up! And besides, birds can't talk.'

'Less of your cheek, if you please, young madam. I'll have you know we seafarers are extremely well acquainted with the habits of ... the stowaway. The hold is a *most* popular hiding place. And they can be wily souls, not above frightening little children into bringing them supplies ...'

'I'm *not* a little child,' said Patch. 'I'm twelve.'

'I don't care if you are twelve or twenty. Something's not right. Let's see then, shall we?' And he turned and started to descend the ladder.

'*Stupido*! Now look what you've gone and done!' hissed Turo.

'Oh, shut up!' said Patch. 'How was I to know?'

She followed Perkins down the ladder. Babette was going to be discovered. And Turo was right. It *would* be her fault. And it was doubly worse because she was a stowaway herself. One stowaway betraying another.

'Who goes there?' Perkins was shouting, as if he was about to catch a burglar. 'Don't think you can hide from me.'

Patch trailed Perkins through the menagerie of

animals, weaving her way between the leopard and the lion and the monkey, following him deeper into the hold. They picked their way past the piles of cases and trunks. Perkins stopped ahead of her. He was breathing heavily.

There was the hatch with 'Ballast, Number Seven' daubed on it in white paint.

But nothing else.

No bag, no coat. No remains of cheese and biscuits. No orange peel.

No Babette.

The hold shivered and creaked and gave a triumphant groan.

Perkins's whiskery face screwed itself into an almighty scowl.

'What's your name?' he barked. 'I'll see to it your parents know about this.'

'But I'm not doing anything wrong!' cried Patch. 'When did getting lost with a jug of beef tea become a crime?'

'I asked you before and I will ask you again,' said Perkins in a threatening manner that Patch didn't care for in the least. He twiddled his moustache and glared at her. '*What* is your name?'

The old Patch would've yelled. She might even have

thrown a punch. She would definitely have hurled the worst insult she could think of at him.

But Lilian had said she mustn't draw attention to herself. And besides, she didn't want to get Turo into trouble.

Stay in character, Patch, she told herself. You are rich and your very fine family lives in Mayfair.

'Chief Steward, I suggest you treat me with a little more respect!' she declared, giving him the full benefit of her hardest stare. 'If you must know, I am Patchouli Cooper-Gordon, and I think my parents will be *extremely* upset when they hear how rude you've been. Now if you'll excuse me, I'll bid you good day!'

Chapter Thirteen

S he was almost at the gate that separated third class from first when she realised that Turo was racing to catch up with her.

'Patch, wait!'

She didn't know why he was looking so worried. It was a stroke of luck that Babette had done a disappearing act. She wondered what would have happened if she'd still been down there, surrounded by all her supplies and disguises. Patch was pretty certain her game would've been up.

The ship lurched and she braced herself, waiting for the rocking to subside. She was still clutching the jug of beef tea, its contents considerably diminished, much of it having sloshed over the sides during her grand exit. It was probably stone-cold by now.

'Patch, do you realise what you've just done?' Turo gasped. His cheeks were pink and his face was stuck in the most awful frown.

'Put that man in his place, I hope!' she said.

'No!' Turo groaned. 'Haven't you heard of a passenger list?'

'What are you talking about?'

'The passenger list. Every ship has one. And every registered passenger is on it. First, second, third class. And on top of that, there are separate lists for the crew.'

In a flash, Patch saw her mistake.

'You mean, everyone is on it except the Cooper-Gordons?' she said. She'd thought she was being so clever, but in fact she'd just been stupid. Or *stupido* as Turo would say.

'Exactly,' said Turo. 'And he didn't believe you. I saw it in his eyes.'

Patch could've kicked herself. Somehow she had to make her wrong a right, and quickly.

'Where is it?' she demanded.

'Where's what?'

'The passenger list of course! Where's it kept?'

'In the purser's bureau. He – the purser – needs it for

when the passengers want to send wireless messages, or deposit jewels and stuff in the safe.'

'And do you think Perkins *will* check?' She didn't even know why she was asking. The man was a terrier. He was the sort of person who wouldn't let anything go.

'He's a vindictive fella,' said Turo. 'He's probably on his way there now, and when he finds out . . .'

'He won't find out,' said Patch with a determination that surprised even herself.

'Whaddaya mean he won't find out?'

'Because we're going to get there first,' she said.

If Turo could just show her where the purser's bureau was, she'd find a way to steal that passenger list and hide it before Perkins had a chance to discover the truth.

'Are you serious?' Turo said incredulously.

'Deadly,' said Patch.

She was determined to thwart Perkins. She didn't like him one bit. He was definitely a child-hater.

And what with Mr Reynolds, that made two.

* * *

The purser's bureau was on the shelter deck, next to the barber's shop and opposite the telephone exchange. Turo knew the nooks and crannies of the ship even better than Lilian. Patch followed him up a series of back staircases and along a warren of corridors, past the firemen's dining room and the second-class dining room and then the officers' mess. Everywhere was still eerily empty.

'You're lucky the weather's so bad,' whispered Turo as he flattened himself against a wall and indicated that Patch peer round the corner. She caught a glimpse of a long, polished wood counter, with a bell to ring for service, and behind it, a series of busy-looking pigeonholes.

'There's usually a queue a mile long of people wanting to send telegrams or drop off valuables,' Turo whispered as Patch drew back.

Valuables! Patch's fingers went to the ribbon at her neck. She felt for her lucky ring. Rubbed the band of gold. Twiddled the stone.

Could it help her now?

A man appeared behind the counter, moving about in an efficient manner, sorting out his papers and lining up his pens.

'Do you know where it'll be?' she whispered. 'The list?' She could see there were all sort of books and ledgers and important-looking papers stacked in the pigeonholes.

'Yes,' murmured Turo. The man disappeared through a door behind the counter and Turo stepped out into the open. 'It's that dark-blue book, see?'

He was pointing at the top shelf on the left-hand side. It was quite high up. He would have to jump. But he looked like he'd be good at jumping.

'If I distract him, can you get it?' she asked.

'I sure can try,' said Turo.

Patch stepped up to the counter, stood the jug of beef tea between her feet and rang the bell. It gave a jaunty ding.

The ship trembled. A little splosh of beef tea landed on her leg. The door behind the counter opened and the purser emerged. He gave her a pleasant smile.

'How can I help you, miss?'

'I wanted to ask about putting this in the safe.' She untied the ribbon from around her neck, slid the ring off it and passed it over to the man.

She was aware that Turo had crawled under the counter. The ring gleamed in the purser's hand. She could just about make out the engraving on the inside. E. & E.

'We usually ask that the more precious items are left in their boxes, especially if they are small like this – do you not have the box, miss?'

The box! She'd forgotten all about it, but she remembered it now. Turquoise with a crimson velvet interior. Had she left it in Miss Alice's rooms? No! She'd shoved it in the pocket of her dress. The red dress that had been kicked under Lilian's bed.

Her heart gave a little skip. She hadn't examined the box properly. It might contain some sort of clue about the origins or intention of the ring.

'I do have one,' she said. 'I'll have to pop back down to get it.' Her eyes flitted briefly beyond the man to Turo jumping up, once, twice, his fingertips reaching out, grazing the edge of the dark blue ledger.

The ship gave another lurch. Turo stumbled. A pile of papers crashed to the floor.

The purser wheeled round.

'Lad, what on earth are you doing?' Turo, regaining his footing, blushed red and opened and closed his mouth like a fish. 'Chief steward sent me ... He wants ...'

Oh dear. Patch could see that Turo wasn't as good as she was at talking herself out of a tricky situation. She would have to help.

Quick as a flash, she stooped, picked up the jug and tossed the remains of the beef tea across the counter.

'Oh no!' she yelped.

The purser whirled round and stared in horror as the brown liquid pooled out around his papers and pens.

Turo did a massive leap, grabbed the ledger and stuffed it under his jumper.

'I'm *so* terribly sorry!' said Patch. 'I didn't mean...'

She plucked her ring from the man's hand. It spun in her palm and the ruby seemed to give her a conspiratorial wink.

'Boy, get a bucket and clean this up!' the purser said sharply. His attention was focused entirely on rescuing the things that were drowning in the muddy beef tea.

'I'll come back with the box then,' said Patch. Behind the man, Turo gave her the thumbs up and she ran.

* * *

Now the ship had stopped tossing and turning and the lurches had subsided to swells, the upper deck was waking up. Passengers with pale faces and set jaws began to creep gingerly out of their state rooms. They took the careful steps of the recently sick.

Patch smiled at them sympathetically. She was happy. Her plan had worked! Turo had managed to swipe the passenger list. She knew she could count on him to hide it somewhere safe. And when Perkins went hunting for it, he wouldn't find it.

He'd never know she wasn't who she claimed to be.

Patch swung the empty beef tea jug from hand to hand. She felt light and carefree. She was safe for now. She could settle in and enjoy the journey. Look forward to seeing Pavlova!

But at the entrance to Lilian's cabin she paused. The door was ajar. That was odd – she was sure she'd shut it earlier. Maybe Lilian was up and about too. But just as she was about to stride in, something made her stop. She could hear voices. Low ones. And through the crack in the door she could see Esty sitting on Lilian's bed, speaking quietly, urgently.

'Why do you always have to be the centre of attention Lil – it's not a game!'

'I know Esty! But it was just so boring before!'

The ship rolled a fraction and the door opened wide. Esty and Lilian both looked up, Esty's face pink, Lilian's closed.

'Sorry,' said Patch, feeling awkward as they continued to stare at her, seemingly at a loss for words. 'Did I interrupt something?'

Had Esty just called Lilian Lil? Wasn't that a bit familiar? But then again, Patch reminded herself,

Esty had looked after Lilian for at least half a dozen journeys. During that time they must have grown quite fond of each other, just like her and Meg.

'No, you haven't interrupted us at all,' said Esty firmly, hurrying to her feet and smoothing down her skirt. 'She's all yours.'

'What was all that about? Does she know about me?' asked Patch as soon as Esty had gone. She was used to people having whispered conversations about her, plotting ways to pass her on. But Lilian was her friend. She wouldn't do that. Would she?

'No, of course not,' said Lilian. 'It's just Esty being Esty. Don't worry about it. It's nothing to do with you.'

A book lay on the floor next to the bed. Patch stooped to pick it up. She recognised it as the same one that Lilian had been reading earlier. On the cover it said Liverpool Elementary School.

'Give that to me Patch, please,' said Lilian.

'But what—'

'It belongs to one of Mrs Chilkes's grandchildren,' said Lilian hurriedly. 'I just borrowed it so that I can keep up with my studies . . .'

Lilian was blushing. She was embarrassed, Patch realised. Quietly Patch placed the book on the bedside table but inside she burned with the injustice of it all.

Lilian's parents were so anti-education she was reduced to poring over other people's discarded textbooks! It wasn't fair.

Lilian sank back down and closed her eyes. With her long golden hair fanning out all over the pillow and her hand to her forehead, she looked like a heroine in a fairy tale.

Except a modern one who wore spectacles. And was really clever.

'Did you give the tea to Babette?' she asked, opening her eyes a fraction.

'She wasn't there,' admitted Patch. 'And then the ship was so unsteady it slopped out.'

All of a sudden she knew she mustn't worry Lilian about the passenger list or Perkins just now. Lilian had warned and warned Patch about the chief steward and his reputation for making trouble. She didn't want to disappoint her. Not while she was sick.

Instead she knelt and rummaged under the bed.

'What are you doing? Oh! I still feel awful.'

'Hold on, just finding...'

Patch fished out the dress. It was covered in dust balls. She dug her hand deep inside the pocket and there it was, the box, just where she'd left it.

'Lilian, look! How could I have forgotten? The ring

was in this box when I found it. Perhaps there's a clue inside. About whether one of the Es is me.'

Lilian opened one eye, like a cat. 'Look inside then.'

Patch opened the box.

The bottom half was all plush crimson velvet where the ring had nestled.

The top half was covered in white satin and there was something printed on the inside of the lid.

She turned the box upside down so she could read it. In gold script were the words:

Tiffany & Co.
New York

'Well?' said Lilian.

'It's the name of the jeweller. Tiffany & Co – and guess what? It's in New York!'

The ring hailed from the exact same city that she was heading towards. What luck! If she could visit the shop she'd be able to find out who E. & E. were.

'Have you heard of them? Tiffany & Co?' she asked Lilian.

'There are scores of jewellery stores in New York. Isn't there an address?'

'No,' said Patch. She jumped back up. The ship hadn't pitched for a good few minutes. She peered out of the porthole. The rain was no longer lashing against the glass and the sky was a paler shade of grey.

There must be *someone* on this ship who had heard of Tiffany & Co, even if Lilian hadn't.

'I'm going outside for a bit,' she said, picking up her skates. 'Do you want to come? It might make you feel better.' She stuck out an elbow helpfully. 'You can lean on me!'

Lilian moaned and turned over. 'No, you go,' she said. 'I honestly don't feel like I'll ever be well again!'

Chapter Fourteen

Up on the boat deck the sea still rose in huge swells but the eye of the storm had passed. Patch had only just buckled up her skates when a small but hefty white being bounded up to her. A square snout bumped against her ankles. It was Sid.

'Sid! What are you doing out here all alone?' she asked, lugging him up. She could feel his heart pounding against hers, boom, boom, boom. His body was warm and hard-muscled. He gave a happy little quiver.

'Poor June will be wondering where you are.' The regal suites were on the promenade deck, the next level down, and forward rather than aft. He was miles from home!

But then she heard a shout and, further down the deck, saw a familiar figure waving. It was June herself, sitting at a table in the Verandah Café. Patch hurried towards her. The café was an elegant place, open on all sides, but with the bonus of a roof so that passengers there could enjoy the view whatever the weather.

'Coo-ee! You found him! Oh you are a nuisance, Sid. Running away from me like that!'

The dog grumbled as Patch passed him over, but June held him fast on her lap. 'He can't resist stretching his legs ... and he's been cooped up for ages because of the weather.'

Sid whined and threw Patch a beseeching look.

'Oh, do stop playing up, Sid,' June said. 'He's spoiled. Give him an inch and he'll take a mile.'

Patch didn't agree that pets could be spoiled. She thought they deserved every ounce of love they could get. But she liked June. She liked her gold tooth that winked when she talked and the violet lenses of her spectacles that lent her a mysterious air. Today she was wearing a hefty rope of pearls round her neck and a large brooch studded with emeralds. Perhaps *she* would know where Tiffany & Co was.

June patted the seat opposite her, a wicker affair

made comfortable with plump cushions. 'On your own? Where's Lilian? Fancy an ice?'

'Yes, please,' said Patch sitting down with her roller skates still on. 'Lilian's sick. She's acting like she's never going to be well again.'

When the ice came, it was delicious, raspberry flavoured and served in a cut-glass bowl with a silver stem. Patch could easily have eaten half a dozen of them but instead she set the dish aside, dug down the front of her dress and pulled out the ring.

'What's that you've got there?' asked June. She leaned forward, her hand reaching out.

'My ring,' said Patch. It was warm where it had been nestling against her skin. Not for the first time she felt as though she and it belonged together. 'I wondered if you might be able to help me find out more about it . . .'

'Where d'you get it?' asked June. A weak ray of sun cut through the grey clouds and for a brief moment her glasses glinted.

'It was . . . a present,' said Patch. She untied the ribbon, slid the ring off and passed it over to June. There was no need to tell the whole story.

'Well,' said June, 'you came to the right person. I know a thing or two about jewellery.' She took the ring between her thumb and forefinger and examined it closely.

'Can I?' she asked, indicating that she would like to try it on.

'Uh … yes,' said Patch, although she was itching to get it back.

June slipped the ring onto her little finger.

'This is the real thing,' she declared authoritatively. 'Good quality gold and a precious gem.'

'It's from a place called Tiffany & Co,' said Patch.

'Is it really? Well, I never,' June regarded her keenly. 'And it's a present you say?'

'Yes. Have you heard of it?'

'Of course I have! Where d'you think I got these?' she rattled her pearls. 'It's on Fifth Avenue – recently moved, used to be on Broadway. My goodness it's a wonderful place. Looks like a Venetian palace. Cost over a million dollars to build.'

'Fifth Avenue?' The words hovered in the air. That was the same street Lilian lived on, wasn't it? But then why had she said she didn't know where it was? Why would she lie about something like that?

There was bound to be a rational explanation. She had probably got muddled up because she was sick.

Patch held out her hand for the ring. Slowly June

slid it off her finger and passed it back.

'You need to keep that safe, young lady.'

Carefully Patch strung the ring back on the ribbon and tied it round her neck.

'Thank you, June,' she smiled and felt a little fizz in her chest.

She was one step closer to finding out who E. & E. were, and if the ring really was hers.

* * *

When the bugle rang for dinner, Patch slipped out of the cabin. Esty would arrive at any minute and she wouldn't be too happy to find Patch still hanging around. She and Lilian had agreed that she should lurk about for a bit up on deck and then come back when the coast was clear.

'Stay out of everyone's way,' reminded Lilian. 'And remember to watch out for the chief steward.'

As Patch approached the grand staircase, she thought about Lilian's reaction to the news that Tiffany & Co was on Fifth Avenue. There had been an awkward silence, and then Lilian had laughed and her eyes had widened behind her spectacles, and she'd said, 'How stupid of me, Patch. It's the seasickness – it does something to your brain.'

And Patch had laughed too, but then she'd asked Lilian if she would accompany her to the shop when they got to New York, and her friend had gone all quiet again and said, 'Of course,' in a way that hadn't sounded convincing at all.

Lilian was being ever so peculiar. Something didn't add up. But what?

It was to do with her parents, Patch was sure of it. They sounded suspicious. They didn't let their daughter go to school. They sent her all the way across the Atlantic on her own. They liked to keep her hidden away.

Patch decided that when she got back to the cabin she was going to ask Lilian outright what was going on. She suspected Lilian was in a pickle and maybe she could help her. Meg had always said that a problem shared was a problem halved.

At the foot of the grand staircase Patch stopped. The doors to the dining saloon were still open. She could see straight in to the lower floor. And something was different. There were four people sitting at their table. Jimmy, Mr Reynolds, June and ... who was that? A strange woman was sitting in Lilian's seat. Her back was to Patch. She didn't have a hat on. It wasn't Mrs Reynolds. She had a cloud of long black hair.

The woman turned towards June and laughed.

Babette?! Decked out in all her finery and looking as though she was perfectly at home.

Patch peered around the rest of the room. She hadn't planned to eat in the saloon because it seemed like too much of a risk. But she couldn't *see* Perkins. Should she chance it? She thought she would. Lilian needn't know.

'Patchouli!' said June as she sank into her seat. 'Meet Mrs Smythe. There's been a right old mix-up with the tables, and as I know poor Lilian has been struck down with *mal de mer*, I suggested she take her place ...'

'Pleased to meet you,' said Patch as though she had never set eyes on Babette before. Mrs Smythe! The name must be part of her disguise.

Babette responded with a gracious nod and a penetrating gaze. She looked even more beautiful than she had in the hold, her heavy black hair swept up and pinned in place with jewel-studded combs. She didn't look a bit ill any more either; she was positively glowing with good health.

Opposite, Mr Reynolds tapped cigar ash into his empty soup bowl.

'No Mrs R today?' enquired Jimmy.

'Headache,' replied Mr Reynolds curtly. 'Lying down.' His eyes met Patch's and for an instant she felt a glimmer of fear. His gaze was startlingly blue. No warmth at all.

When she was sure that June was safely engrossed in conversation with Jimmy, and Mr Reynolds had stalked off to get more cigars, Patch moved closer to Babette.

'Where were you this afternoon?' she murmured. 'I got into terrible trouble delivering you your beef tea.'

'Oh darling, that *was* kind. But the storm quite brought me back to life! I was on deck!'

'On deck?' Patch looked at her aghast, remembering the violent pitching of the boat, the giant waves that were surely the height of skyscrapers. 'Was that safe?'

'It was marvellous!' said Babette quietly, her eyes dancing. 'I rushed about helping the sailors and then I searched out the snuggest corner and set up camp. Tell me, who *is* that nasty-looking specimen opposite? I wouldn't trust him an inch.'

At last, someone who understood, someone who instinctively knew, just like Patch did, that there was something indefinably bad about Mr Reynolds.

'Mr Reynolds,' said Patch watching him as he finished berating a waiter and slunk back into his seat. 'I suspect he is an awful child-hater. *And* woman-hater. Avoid him at all costs.'

'And what about her?' Babette's gaze slid towards June, still deep in conversation with Jimmy.

'Oh, that's June, she's fine,' said Patch, thinking of the Genoese fancies and the ice cream.

'Really?' asked Babette. 'I don't think her dog would agree.'

What did Babette mean? It was true that Sid wasn't sitting on June's lap tonight. Instead he was crouched under the table. He saw Patch looking at him, scrabbled to his feet and trotted over to arrange himself next to her chair. She leaned down and patted him on the head.

'You're happy, aren't you?' she whispered to him. Was he?

'You then,' said Babette, looking carefully at Patch. 'Something tells me you're not who you say you are.'

'Sssh!' said Patch. Her eyes flitted around the table. But Jimmy and June were still chatting away nineteen to the dozen and Mr Reynolds was entirely focused on his food.

'You mustn't tell anyone!'

'As if I would! Don't worry, your secret is safe with me – just as mine is with you. I had my suspicions as soon as I saw you in the hold.'

'Did you?' whispered Patch. She watched Mr

Reynolds lay his cane on the table, saw how the silver tip caught the lights of the chandeliers. Was he listening? No, they were talking so quietly there was no way he'd be able to hear amidst the chatter of the other guests. 'It happened by accident. Me, hiding on this boat. How could you tell?'

'I can spot a fellow stowaway a mile off!' said Babette, keeping her voice low. 'It's a look and you've got it. And I must say, you seem to be doing a jolly good job of fitting in. Although hand on heart, you could do with a disguise or two ...'

But Patch had stopped listening. Across the room a figure approached. Fingers twiddling ginger-coloured whiskers, beady little eyes surveying the scene. Their eyes met. A gleam of recognition. He reached into his pocket and held up a piece of paper.

Inwardly, she cursed herself for risking the dining room. She had to be quicker, sharper, more like Babette.

Abruptly Patch pushed her chair back. 'Sorry,' she said to the table in general, 'I've got to ...'

She turned and half walked, half ran from the room, weaving her way between the crowded tables, past the silks and the satins, through the clouds of perfume.

'Are you all right, miss?' It was Matty blocking the

doorway, bearing a platter of jewel-coloured jellies and crystallised fruits. He glanced behind her, saw Perkins. 'I think the chief steward might—'

'I'm fine,' she said, elbowing her way past him. 'Just going to check on Lilian.' But it was too late. A hand had already clamped down on her shoulder, insistent fingers curling into a pincer-like grip.

'Know this young lady, do you?' Perkins asked Matty. And to Patch he said, 'Like to introduce me to your parents, would you? The *Cooper-Gordons*?'

'The passenger list ...' she faltered. How could he know? Turo had taken it. She'd seen him stuff it under his jumper. He was meant to have hidden it. She'd trusted him!

'Mysteriously disappeared from the purser's bureau,' Perkins completed the sentence for her. His whiskers quivered. 'Luckily, I keep a spare.' He waved the sheet of paper at her again.

'Now, tell me again. Your name?'

She didn't know why he was asking. It was obvious he knew she was a fraud. There was only one thing for it.

With a twist and a jab, she jerked out of his grasp. Took a step backwards. Saw a red rush of anger flood his face.

Like a boxer, she danced away from him, darting this way and that, and before he could grab her, she had turned and sprinted up the grand staircase, her feet barely touching the steps. Round and round, past the shelter deck, past the promenade deck – and she could hear him following her, shouting, 'You won't get away from me.'

And then she was outside on the boat deck and the night was black and the moon was high, and she was tearing at the canvas of the nearest lifeboat, hauling herself in and dropping down and slapping the canvas back in place. Quiet, quiet, she tried to still her breath, listening as the door slammed and Perkins burst out, his footsteps loud, then dwindling. Which way had he gone? Forward or aft?

She couldn't stay here. He was the sort of person who wouldn't give up. Sooner or later he'd be back. He'd know the lifeboats were an obvious place to hide.

She stood, ready to pull herself out. But then the door slammed again. The stamp of more footsteps. And this time, voices. Patch froze.

'It's a gift horse, I tell you!'

It was Mr Reynolds. She shivered. She'd recognise that voice anywhere. Smooth but with a gravelly undertone. He must be standing right by the lifeboat.

'Little rich girl ... all on her lonesome ... parents back in Blighty ...'

It was hard to hear over the constant tremors and trembles of the ship. But those few words were enough to startle Patch and make her strain to hear more. Rich girl? Parents back in Blighty?

Was he talking about Lilian?

'You heard her – "Fifteen bedrooms and an oak-floored ballroom."' Mr Reynolds had put on a high falsetto voice. Patch burned. He *was* talking about Lilian! Mimicking her.

'A nice little earner while we set up operations on Fifth Avenue.'

'But what if the coppers are already on to us?' Another voice, also male. Younger, with a rough edge.

An exasperated grunt. And then, 'Have I taught you nothing? Think of our reputations! We take advantage when opportunities present themselves. Strike while the iron is hot!'

'But ...'

Patch strained to hear what the second man was saying. He wasn't nearly so clear. Must be further away. Or downwind. But she knew this much: whatever it was Mr Reynolds was planning, this other man didn't seem as keen.

'For God's sake man. De Haviland is worth millions! New money and lots of it. Think of the ransom!' It was Mr Reynolds again. 'If we play our cards right, we'll make a fortune.'

'We need to watch out for that whiny brat though, can't have her reporting her friend missing until we're off the ship.'

'Won't happen. If she gets in the way, she's out of the picture. No one's going to notice a disappeared kid.'

The hairs on Patch's arms prickled. Whiny brat? Disappeared kid? Was he talking about *her*? And if he was, did that mean he knew she was on the boat all alone?

She thought back to the first day when they'd had that brief encounter by the lifeboat. She'd been too quick to convince herself that he hadn't seen or suspected anything. But now a more sinister thought presented itself. Had he known she was a stowaway all along? But decided to keep quiet for his own nefarious reasons?

She felt a swell of anger. She hated to be wrong-footed. She wanted to burst out of the lifeboat, grab that silly cane he carried and hit him with it, hard. But besides the anger, she was scared. Out of the picture? What did that mean?

Instinct told her to stay put. Keep quiet, keep safe, for now.

She'd thought that Mr Reynolds was just a common child-hater, like many of the other adults she had met in her short life. But this was worse. Much worse. This was *dangerous*. Ransoms meant kidnappings. Usually of rich people. Rich people like Lilian.

Mr Reynolds and his mystery friend were plotting to kidnap her friend. And what were they going to do with *her*? If she got in their way? What did 'disappear' her mean?

Scrunched up in the darkness, Patch waited for the voices to fade and the footsteps to disappear to nothing.

She had to warn Lilian, alert the captain. It didn't matter that her cover would be blown.

But she also had to be careful. If they saw her, who was to say they wouldn't just hurl her straight overboard?

Cautiously, Patch lifted the canvas. She couldn't see a thing. But they couldn't be very far away, could they? Heart thumping, she climbed back out of the boat and dropped down to the dark deck. And ... What was *that*? Something nudged at her foot. Something snuffling, something ... alive? She took a step back, but the thing did a sort of excited grunt and followed her. The hairs on the back of her neck spiked. The thing brushed against her leg again and she felt the flick of a tail against her ankles.

Was it true that at sea there were rats the size of cats? She opened her mouth to scream . . .

Chapter Fifteen

And closed it again.

It was miles too big for a rat. Teeth had not been bared, nor had claws scratched. Whatever it was, it wasn't in a hurry to attack.

Slowly, she stretched out a hand.

The creature pushed its body against hers, emitting a loud grunt, and then all in a rush she felt its thick-set, squat shape, and saw its square snout and its gleaming eyes, and smelled the aroma of ginger biscuits.

'Sid!' breathed Patch. A great rush of relief. An excited bark.

'Ssshhh! What are you doing up here?' she whispered.

She scratched him behind the ears. He nuzzled her and snorted happily.

June's regal suite was the floor below. Sid must've scampered after her when she'd escaped the dining saloon. Gently, Patch patted the dog to keep him quiet, and then, taking great care to stay hidden in the shadow of the lifeboat, peered further up the deck. She could just about discern two shapes. They had stopped. But it was too dark to see if they were looking her way.

Quickly Patch scooped Sid up and charged back through the door. She would drop the dog off on the promenade deck and, fingers crossed, he would find his way home. Then she'd find Lilian and tell her everything *she* had just heard.

Dinner had finished. Passengers thronged the staircase, calling out to each other, making plans to meet in the lounge or the smoking room or the library. But no one paid any attention to the lone girl and a snuffling dog.

* * *

'Lilian!'

The cabin was dark. Patch clicked on the bedside

lamp. Lilian was curled up in a ball. She shook her shoulder. 'Wake up!'

'Gerr-off,' mumbled Lilian.

'No, Lilian, you must wake up!'

Reluctantly Lilian opened her eyes, blinking in the light. Her cheeks were flushed a pale pink. She looked oddly vulnerable without her spectacles on.

'I was asleep! What d'you want?'

'You've got to get up,' urged Patch. 'We have to go and see the captain now.'

'What are you talking about?'

Patch took a deep breath. There was so much to say, she didn't know where to start.

'Lilian, listen. It's Mr Reynolds. He's got a plan. A terrible one! He's going to *kidnap* you.' The words were coming out so fast they were tripping over one another. 'And he's going to "*disappear*" me, whatever that means . . .' She frantically tried to formulate everything she'd heard.

The pink had disappeared. Lilian stared at Patch. She grappled for her spectacles and shoved them on. She seemed to be at a loss for words.

'It's not true,' she said eventually.

'It is true!' Why was Lilian taking so long to understand?

'I just *heard* them plotting it with my very own ears! Mr Reynolds and another man, I don't know who. But Mr Reynolds said, "If we play our cards right, we'll make a fortune." That's why we have to go and see the captain!'

'We can't.' Lilian blinked furiously. She looked like a frightened rabbit.

'What? Of course we can!'

There was a pause. Patch could almost see Lilian's thoughts whirring around inside her head but she couldn't quite read them. It *looked* like she was trying to decide what to say next.

'Because of *you*, you ninny!' she said at last. 'They'll find out about you.'

'Oh, that doesn't matter now!' Patch cried. She didn't understand why Lilian hadn't grasped how real and dangerous this threat was. 'This is miles bigger than that!'

Lilian shook Patch's hand off her arm. Her face had the closed-up look again.

'Are you still ill?' asked Patch. 'Is that it? Then I'll go on my own.' She started for the door.

'Stop!' Lilian looked stricken. Behind the spectacles her black eyes bored holes into Patch's as though she were pinning her to the spot. 'Don't go. You'll spoil everything. Please!'

'Spoil what?' asked Patch, confused. Something had gone wrong. Something she didn't understand. Why wasn't Lilian relieved? Why was she pleading with Patch to say nothing?

'Patch, just forget everything you've heard. I'd rather you didn't breathe a word.'

Patch stared at her. Watched as Lilian came to some sort of decision.

'Patch, if you say anything, I swear I will never, ever, speak to you again.'

Patch took a step back. Where had *her* Lilian gone? Her *friend* Lilian? Clever, funny, kind Lilian? This Lilian was someone entirely different.

'Do you *want* to be kidnapped?'

'Of course not! Oh,' Lilian almost wailed, 'I wish I'd never set eyes on you!'

'What?' Patch's voice rose. She was starting to feel angry now. 'Mr Reynolds, the man who *you* thought was utterly charming, is not. He is going to kidnap you! All because you can't keep your mouth shut. Boasting about your la-di-da mansion on fancy Fifth Avenue—'

'I did *not* boast,' said Lilian coldly. 'And ...' She stared at Patch for a horribly heavy moment before continuing. 'You are stubborn. And you don't listen.

No wonder your relatives passed you around like a parcel.'

Patch gasped. She felt like she had been kicked in the chest. Hot tears pricked at her eyes. She blinked and clenched her fists. She would not cry in front of this new Lilian.

'Come out, I know you're in there!' Someone was hammering on the door.

'It's Perkins!' said Patch. He must've been hiding on the boat deck, seen her climb out of the lifeboat and followed her back down. 'Lilian, please,' she implored, 'you're in danger, we *have* to tell—'

'Don't answer it!' said Lilian. She had gone quite still.

Patch hesitated. Lilian was being horrible. Incomprehensible. If she'd heard the way those men had talked about her she'd be as frightened as Patch was.

'I'm not going anywhere until you open up!' came the voice from outside, accompanied by more hammering.

Patch gave Lilian a last, anguished glance. If she wasn't going to protect herself, then Patch would have to do it for her.

'I wish you'd understand I'm doing this for you!' said Patch, and before she could change her mind, she strode over to the door and opened it wide. It *was* Perkins, still clutching his bit of paper, his whiskers waggling.

'I'm glad you've found me,' started Patch, 'because—'

'Patch!' said Lilian warningly.

'Know this young lady, do you?' Perkins had already bustled his way into the cabin. He was addressing Lilian who had turned as white as a sheet. She looked as though she wished the ground would swallow her up. 'She bothering you?'

'Well, since you ask . . .' said Lilian.

'Tell him, Lilian!' Patch waited for her to say the right thing. But Lilian's face was clenched tight. There was a long pause.

'Her name is Patch,' said Lilian, enunciating each word with a kind of dreadful deliberation. 'She shouldn't be here. She's not a registered passenger on the ship.'

Patch stared.

Lilian? Her *friend* Lilian? Betraying her? She didn't understand what was happening.

'I thought as much,' said Perkins, giving his whiskers a victorious twiddle. 'Come on then.' He reached out and grasped Patch by the arm and began to drag her from the room. 'Time for you to meet the captain.'

* * *

The wind moaned and the sea roared as Patch and Perkins scurried along the dark deck to the captain's cabin. Patch shivered. The cold night air pecked at her skin like a hungry hen.

'Let go!' cried Patch. She had to shout to be heard above the din of the boat. Perkins hadn't released his grip the whole way, his fingers pinching so hard it hurt. 'I'm not going to run away again. I'm coming, can't you see?'

Lilian's face kept flashing in front of her, a Lilian she didn't recognise. The closed face. The unexpected reaction. Everything had happened so quickly. She couldn't make sense of it.

'I'm not taking any chances with you,' said Perkins. 'Not after you've spent the whole day dodging me.'

'Can I help you, chief steward?' An officer was blocking their way. He regarded them questioningly.

'I'm here to see Captain Westow, sir,' said Perkins. 'Is he in his quarters?'

'He's at the helm – says not to be disturbed,' replied the officer. 'You can't go up there now. Caught a stowaway?' He cocked his head in Patch's direction.

'Yes, sir,'

'Well done, old chap. I'll get you your grog.'

The officer disappeared for a moment and then

returned with a bottle of amber-coloured liquid which he tossed to the chief steward.

'But *I'd* like to see the captain,' said Patch. 'I've got something to tell him.'

'Did you not hear?' said the officer irritably. 'He is busy. He has a ship to steer. There's no time to waste on a stowaway's sob story.'

'But it's not about ...' The sentence trailed away to nothing. Lilian hadn't wanted Patch's help. She had made that quite clear. And anyway, Patch was beginning to think she didn't deserve it either.

The officer turned back to Perkins. 'Set her to work. She'll have to earn her passage. And I'll tell the captain how helpful you've been.'

* * *

Perkins took Patch all the way down to the lower deck.

'That-a-way,' he said, pointing a wavering finger towards the exact same metal door she'd hidden behind yesterday. He hiccoughed loudly. He'd had a fair few swigs of grog on the way down.

Patch stopped in her tracks. Turned to him in disbelief. She could already hear the noises: the rumbles and clangs and the unearthly shouts. She could feel the heat. Surely he wasn't serious?

'I'm not going down there,' she said stoutly. She thought of Scully and the sweat and the fear and the smell of singed hair. 'You can't make me.'

'Oh, yes I can,' slurred Perkins, giving Patch a little shove. 'Get down there now.' He opened the door and it swung wide.

They were so close she could see the top of the iron ladder. She pictured the furnaces, blazing and burning furiously. Her throat felt sore, the dust already working its way into her lungs.

She'd thought the little house in Lambeth had been the bottom of the staircase. But *this* was the bottom, and not just by a few steps but by about one hundred thousand million. This was the staircase *below* the staircase. Miles worse than anything she had ever experienced before.

The chief steward prodded her again.

Meg had said don't be scared of drunken men. Just one push and they'd fall over.

'I'm not going down there. I'm not!' she shouted. And she shoved back, hard, knocking into Perkins who tottered unsteadily, trying to hold on to her with one hand because his other one was intent on keeping hold of his precious grog.

He couldn't catch her. She was too quick and bashed past him and launched herself away from the hatch, away from hell and then – thud. She had crashed into another human being. Someone tall and stout with an ample chest. Someone with large hands who grasped her firmly by the shoulders and held her at arm's length.

Chapter Sixteen

I t was the woman from the kitchen: Mrs Chilkes. The imposing one who had allowed her to make the beef tea.

'Give her here, she's my stowaway,' blethered Perkins, staggering up behind her. 'She's got to work her passage.'

Mrs Chilkes ignored Perkins and nudged Patch so that she was standing under one of the flickering lights.

'You!' she said. 'I didn't have *you* down for a stowaway. I almost took you for gentry.' Her eyes hardened as another thought struck her. 'All a made-up story was it, filching that beef tea for Esty?'

'No!' said Patch. And in that moment, the

adaptability of her nature took over. She realised that if she were to work her passage, she should at least have some say in the matter. She could clean. She could run errands. She could work in the kitchen . . .

And as soon as she could, she would seek out Lilian and find out what was jolly well going on.

'Mrs Chilkes, can't I help you?' she pleaded. 'I'll be much more useful in the kitchen than in the boiler room. You saw how capable I was this morning. I can cook a chicken. I can peel carrots. I know how to make suet pudding!'

'Oh, you do, do you?' The woman observed her with a practised eye. Assessing her, Patch thought.

'Now look here . . .' began Perkins, the words fading as Mrs Chilkes drew herself up to her full height. She was a very tall lady.

'Chief Steward Perkins!' she barked, 'Captain Westow is cantankerous but not cruel. If he knew you were planning to throw this one down amongst the stokers and the trimmers I believe he'd have a thing or two to say about it.'

She turned back to Patch. Nodded once, twice. Patch held her breath. Crossed her fingers behind her back.

'Truth is, I could use an extra pair of hands in the

kitchen. Fair competent you were this morning.' She took Patch's hand. Her grasp was firm and a bit raspy. 'Perkins, she's coming with me. I'll let the captain know tomorrow.'

* * *

The cabin that Mrs Chilkes marched Patch to was past the storerooms and along a tangle of corridors.

'I dare say you were frightened by what you saw,' said Mrs Chilkes as she bustled along. 'They're fearsome-looking men those stokers and trimmers but they wouldn't do you any harm.'

'No,' agreed Patch, thinking of Scully. She felt in her pocket for the whistle he'd given her. Still there.

Mrs Chilkes pushed open a door leading into a cramped room with six bunks in it, five of them already occupied by gently snoring bodies.

'Lav's that-a-way, young Patchet,' she said, cocking her head further down the passageway. 'And then you'd better get your head down. It's very late – near eleven o clock – and you'll need to be up at five. I won't stand for idle hands tomorrow!'

After Mrs Chilkes had gone, Patch climbed into the empty bunk. Lilian's old-fashioned dress was unbearably hot and all of a sudden she hated it. What had just happened with Lilian? Why had she turned against her? She'd betrayed her, abandoned her just like all her relatives.

Patch felt for the ring on the ribbon round her neck and slid it onto her thumb. There was something about it that was comforting.

E. & E. E. & E. E. & E.

It didn't matter that she had to work her passage. She was still bound for New York. She would still get to visit Tiffany & Co to find out about the ring. She could still see Pavlova dance at the Metropolitan Opera House.

But it wasn't enough.

Try as she might to put Lilian out of her mind, she couldn't. Despite her odd behaviour, despite her rejection of Patch, Lilian, her friend – her erstwhile friend – was still in danger. Why wouldn't, or couldn't, she see that?

As sleep approached, Patch made a decision. Tomorrow she would find Turo. Maybe, together, they could try and work out what was going on.

* * *

But the next day, even though she was desperate to find Turo, she had to wait. The life of a scullion – for that is what she was now – was a hard one, with every minute, every hour occupied. From first thing, when a rough hand shook her awake and Mrs Chilkes told her to 'get out of that silly dress and into your uniform' (a grey dress that was miles too big, with a white apron on top that more or less held everything in place), and all through the morning, during which she peeled three vats of potatoes, scoured an endless mountain of pots and pans, and portioned out one hundred pats of butter into tiny cut-glass dishes ('no more, no less,' said Mrs Chilkes), there was no respite.

By dinner time, which was what the kitchen crew called lunch (well before noon because 'all meals have to be taken before service,' said Mrs Chilkes), Patch's wrists were aching and her fingers were raw and she practically slumped at the table, shovelling down the brown beef and gravy followed by plum pudding.

When the plates had been cleared, Mrs Chilkes announced that she had a new job for her. Could she count?

'Of course!'

Could she write?

'I'm not stupid!'

'Less of your cheek, young Patchet,' said Mrs Chilkes, who seemed to have decided that was her name. She was to go down to the stores and do a cauliflower inventory. 'I need to know if I've got enough to do a cauliflower cheese for first class tonight, and second class tomorrow. Off you go, quick sharp.'

* * *

Patch rushed down to the lower deck and counted the cauliflowers as quickly as she could, and then set off to find Turo. She was getting more and more familiar with the ship's layout: the lifts and the staircases, the passages and corridors, the entrances and the exits.

At last she found him in a tiny cubbyhole just along from the crew's quarters. He was sitting on a low stool next to a line of boots, all waiting to be polished.

As he heard her approach, he turned round. His eyes took in her scullion's outfit and almost popped.

'Patch! Whaddaya doin' in that get-up?'

'Lilian betrayed me,' she said. It sounded dramatic. But in all honesty it *had* been dramatic. 'And Perkins caught me. He knows there are no Cooper-Gordons on the ship.'

'But I took the passenger list!' said Turo. 'How did he know?'

'He had another copy,' she said. 'But that doesn't matter now. So much more has happened. Budge up. I haven't got long.'

Turo made a space for her and she crouched down next to him and told him what she'd heard when she'd been hiding in the lifeboat, and how Lilian had reacted, and how she'd pretty much handed Patch over to Perkins on a plate.

'I know what I heard. A ransom they said. A "nice little earner". But Lilian refused to believe me. She went mad, begging me not to say anything. And I don't understand why. I think she might be hiding something.'

'Holy gee, I don't get why she turned you in,' said Turo. 'She *likes* you, anyone can see that.' He scrunched his face up. 'If she *is* hiding something, maybe she got scared and snitched on you so's she wouldn't get found out.'

Patch thought of Lilian's white face. The way she had sat so still when Perkins had burst into the cabin. It was almost as if she hadn't wanted to be seen.

And it had worked. He *hadn't* really seen her. He'd paid hardly any attention to her at all. He was so intent on catching Patch and winning his grog.

The secret schoolbooks. The hiding out in the cabin.

186

The whisperings with Esty. The ignorance about Tiffany & Co.

'Have you still got that passenger list?' she said.

'It's hidden under my mattress. Why?'

'Get it, please.' An idea was forming in Patch's mind. She remembered Mrs Chilkes saying she was always there for Lilian, 'grog or no grog'. Those had been her exact words.

'Here.' Turo was back, and he was shoving the passenger list into her hands.

There were hundreds of names. All in alphabetical order. Should she look under D or H? De Haviland... her finger ran up and down the pages, searching, searching. She checked again to be sure. A shocked lump wedged itself into the back of her throat.

'It's not just the Cooper-Gordons that are missing,' she said to Turo. 'There's no de Havilands either.'

Turo snatched the list away from her and scanned it furiously.

'Well I never... what's she playin' at?' he said.

'But... why?' Patch's mind ticked over furiously. If Lilian wasn't a de Havilland, then who *was* she? And was *that* why she had behaved so peculiarly?

'I've got to get back to the kitchen,' she said. 'But will you come with me to see Lilian later? To confront her. Find out what's going on?'

'Sure thing. I reckon just before the bugle sounds for dinner the kitchen will be in a frenzy. You should be able to make your escape then.'

* * *

Turo was right. The kitchen *had* been in a frenzy and it was easy to escape unnoticed. Easy to slip past Mrs Chilkes who was busy scolding an assistant cook about a case of burnt milk. She skidded along the corridor, darting between the guests who were heading for the dining saloon. Some of them gave her inquisitive looks but most of them ignored her. Lowly scullions were even less interesting than respectable children.

When she arrived at Lilian's cabin, Turo was waiting.

'Hey kids! Everything tip-top?' It was Jimmy, striding down the corridor resplendent in a plum-coloured suit and smelling of limes. He did a double take when he realised the dishevelled-looking scullion in front of him was actually Patchouli Cooper-Gordon.

'You playin' dress-up?' he asked.

Patch liked Jimmy. He deserved the truth. Hurriedly she explained her predicament. She wasn't a Cooper-Gordon. She was Patch Leonard – not a guest but a stowaway, now working her passage to New York.

'I'll be darned!' said Jimmy delightedly. 'This ship is awash with characters claiming they aren't who they are. Most entertaining! And what's your story?' he asked Turo, who was gazing admiringly at the glamourous gentleman's two-tone brogues.

'Ain't no story,' said Turo. 'I'm a ship boy through and through. And when I'm a grown man I intend to become a captain.'

'Young man, that *is* a story, and a darned good one too.' Jimmy took a shiny coin out of his pocket, flipped it into the air and tossed it at Turo, who caught it with a flourish in one hand.

'And you Patch-the-brave, if I can do anything to help, I'm at your service. Toodle-oo!'

'Toodle-oo,' echoed Patch.

As soon as they heard the elevator doors clang shut they knocked on the cabin door. But there was no answer.

'She must've already gone up,' said Turo.

'Well, I'm going in anyway,' said Patch. She turned the handle on the door. Not locked. Was it wrong to go snooping? Probably, but she didn't care.

The cabin was just as it was when she'd last been there. The desk was covered in a muddle of books and papers: some dog-eared editions of *Girls' Best Friend*, several copies of the ship's newspaper, the *Cunard Daily Bulletin,* and a copy of *The Tale of Tom Kitten*. She took the Beatrix Potter and tucked it under her apron. She was especially fond of Tabitha Twichit and her kittens.

Next she moved on to the trunk at the bottom of the bed, the one emblazoned with 'Lilian de Haviland' in gold letters. It was full of the sort of old-fashioned dresses that Lilian wore all the time – bulky, itchy affairs more suited to the children of bygone days – but that was all.

Meanwhile, Turo investigated the chest of drawers by the bed, but every single drawer was empty. On the dressing table, neatly laid out, were a mother-of-pearl-backed brush, a comb and a mirror, all engraved with the monogram LdH.

Patch lay flat on the floor and peered under the bed. There was the sick bucket, thankfully empty, and next to that her roller skates. Beyond the skates lay the crumple of her red dress . . . and what was that? Right at the back was a battered cardboard suitcase. Patch wriggled further under the bed and stretched to reach it. It was a dusty old thing with a metal clip fastening.

'Giddy up then, what's inside?' asked Turo.

Patch clicked the tab and the suitcase sprang open. It was stuffed to the brim. On top were more comics.

Underneath were several dresses in faded prints. They had been worn many times and Patch could see where they had been 'let out' or patched. At the bottom, tucked in the corner were a pile of old school exercise books. They looked like the one Lilian had been surreptitiously reading the other day. The one that she had said was 'nothing important'.

Patch reached for the one on the top. The front cover read:

LIVERPOOL ELEMENTARY SCHOOL
Junior Arithmetic

Patch flipped it open. On the inside cover, in neat letters was: *This is the property of Lillian Green. Return if found.*

The book underneath was identical, although instead of arithmetic, it was grammar. It was also the property of Lillian Green.

Patch passed the schoolbooks to Turo and then plucked up a cardigan. It was knitted in a heathery-coloured wool and darned at the elbows. On the inside, at the neck were the embroidered initials LG.

'Who *is* Lillian Green?' asked Patch

Behind her the cabin door creaked open.

'It's me.'

Chapter Seventeen

P atch whirled round. Lilian was standing in the doorway. Patch felt her face grow hot. She dropped the cardigan.

'Have you been *lying* to us?' She felt a wave of fury rip through her. After all the truths she'd told Lilian, she'd got a bunch of lies in return.

Lilian's face, which for a brief moment had been defiant, crumpled. She stepped inside the cabin.

'It's all ruined. I'm sorry, Patch.'

'What do you mean it's all ruined?' said Patch.

'And if you're Lillian Green,' cut in Turo, 'who is Lilian de Haviland?'

'Dead?'

'*What?*'

'Oh, I don't know if she's dead or alive!' cried Lillian. She sounded exasperated. 'I don't have a clue who she was *or* is. Except that her trunk was in the Cunard lost property office, and it'd been there, uncollected, for years. It's nothing more than a coincidence that we've got the same name give or take the extra "l".'

Patch's mind whirled. She sat down on the bed with a thump.

'So if you're not *this* Lilian,' said Turo, pointing at the trunk, its contents now spilling all over the floor, 'then none of this stuff belongs to you. You're an imposter! Just like Patch and Babette!'

Lillian blushed a deep, dark red.

'And New York . . .' began Patch.

'There is no house on Fifth Avenue,' said Lillian bluntly. 'No fifteen bedrooms, no ballroom big enough for four hundred guests. There is no Mama and Papa. There is no Lilian de Haviland.'

Patch stared. She looked very hard at the girl standing in front of her, trying to make sense of everything she was saying. Trying to bring her into focus. But it was as though Lillian had turned into a puppet doll and all her limbs were dancing madly, and then they were coming apart: arms, legs, head, body, all severed, nothing matching, nothing fitting. Everything just in a terrible, jumbled muddle.

Proud, brave Lilian, who had crossed the Atlantic on her own multiple times; whose parents didn't seem to care that much for her; who was bold and confident and quick-witted. None of it was real. It had all been a sham.

'Are you actually saying that you made it all up?'

'Yes.'

'But why? Does Esty know she's fetching and carrying for . . .' – Patch picked up the school exercise book again and read the name – 'Lillian Green?'

'Yes, Esty knows,' said Lillian. 'She's my sister.'

'Your sister?' echoed Turo.

Patch remembered the looks that had passed between Lillian and Esty. The irritability, the fondness, the worry. The time she'd heard Esty call Lillian 'Lil.'

Now it all made sense.

'Patch,' appealed Lillian, 'please! I've felt terrible since last night. I was scared out of my wits and I didn't know what to do. When Perkins asked if I knew you, I panicked. I couldn't have his attention on me. I had a split second to choose between protecting you or my sister. I chose Esty. If she's found out she'll lose her job. And it would all be my fault.'

Patch noticed that the peculiar-sounding half British

half American accent had gone. Lillian was beginning to sound much more ordinary. Much more ... like a girl from Liverpool.

She had thought *she* was the one with a talent for acting.

'But you were mean!' Patch said angrily. She felt cheated. 'You said that you could understand why everyone passed me on like a parcel!'

The hurt was still raw.

Now Lillian looked up sharply. 'And I told *you* to avoid the chief steward at all costs. I couldn't have him anywhere near me. But did you listen? No. You went about dancing, drawing attention to yourself, and then you brought him straight to this cabin!'

'But that was because—'

'Hang on,' interrupted Turo. 'Why did you think up this whole charade in the first place?' he asked Lillian.

'Do you want to know, Patch?' Lillian tried to catch Patch's eye.

'Yes,' said Patch. She wouldn't look at Lillian. She couldn't.

'Our granny brought us up because our mam and our da died when we were very young,' Lillian began. 'When Esty was old enough, she went into service, and a bit later she got a job here, on this ship. For as long as I can remember, Esty wanted to work at sea. Ever since she was young she'd go down to the docks and dream about it. We lost count of the letters she wrote to the secretaries of the shipping companies enquiring for positions vacant.'

Lillian paused, sat down on the bed next to Patch. Their elbows were almost touching. Patch jumped up and went to stand next to Turo. Lillian looked at them both beseechingly. 'You don't know how hard it is to get a position as a stewardess! But Esty did it. And we were all so happy for her.'

Lillian's expression fell. She pressed her knuckles to her eyes. 'But then ...' A long, shuddery sigh. 'Granny died late last year.'

'I'm sorry,' said Turo. Patch said nothing. She heard Lillian sniff. Despite her best efforts, she felt herself start to thaw.

'The landlord took the house back, wanted it for *his* family.' Now Patch did look up. Lillian's eyes were very bright. Two pink spots bloomed on her cheeks. 'I'd won a place at the Liverpool Institute High School for Girls. I was meant to start in January. I was so looking forward to it!'

'The school that I was meant to go to?' Patch shook her head in disbelief. Finally the fog was starting to clear. No wonder Lillian had been so interested in that part of her story.

'Yes, Patch. I had dreamed of going for so long! And Granny was so proud. I was going to study French and Latin, history, mathematics, philosophy, chemistry – can you imagine? I was interviewed by Miss Alice Grey.'

'*My* Alice Grey?' said Patch.

'Yes! She said that if I was successful in the local examinations, I could eventually go to university and then have a career ... as a scientist or a foreign correspondent or a teacher ...'

'Well, why didn't you go then?' asked Patch. It came out sounding cross. But it wasn't meant to. Patch was confused. And her questions needed answers.

Now Lillian really did look exasperated. 'Oh, Patch! We're poor! Don't you see? I was accepted as a day girl!' she said. 'If everything had stayed the same, I would've attended while living at home with Granny. But after she died there *was* no home. The only possible way would've been to board – and how do you imagine we could've afforded that?'

She put her head in her hands. And then she said, her voice muffled, 'Esty didn't know what to do with me. She panicked and came up with this plan. Says it's just a "temporary measure". Just until she and Matty – he's her fiancé – come up with a better idea.'

'And you've been living on the ship for how long?' said Turo.

'Since just after Christmas,' said Lillian.

'Woah!' Turo whistled.

'Mrs Chilkes knows, and Matty knows, and Mr Edgar – the chief steward before Perkins – he knew,' said Lillian. 'Otherwise, we'd never have been able to carry it off.'

'What do you mean, carry it off?'

'Mr Edgar was the one who told us if there were any spare cabins,' Lillian said. 'But now he's retired and this is Perkins's first crossing. We took a chance on this cabin – Matty found out it was unoccupied – and hoped that Perkins might not notice. Mrs Chilkes says he's out to prove himself, warned us we'd have to watch out for him. So do you see? I can't be discovered! I can't have Esty and Matty lose their jobs!'

Patch's hunch had been right. She remembered Mrs Chilkes's cryptic comment – 'I'm always here for Esty and her girl, grog or no grog.'

At the time, Patch had assumed Mrs Chilkes was referring to her, that somehow she'd guessed *she* was a stowaway. But instead, Mrs Chilkes had been saying the promise of grog would never tempt her to hand over Lillian.

'But you could've said!' Patch burst out. 'Right from the start I told you *everything* about me!'

She remembered that first exchange of stories in the lifeboat. Hers had been the truth, but Lillian's had been a gigantic fib.

'I'd been so lonely,' said Lillian miserably. 'Shut away in this cabin and always having to creep around. And then when you came, I saw how we could do things together, be a cover for each other.'

'Like going to the dining saloon you mean,' said Patch bitterly. She recalled how eager Lillian had been that first night, going up to the restaurant.

No wonder she hadn't known which cutlery to use.

'Well, yes, there was that,' admitted Lillian. 'But also I wanted to be part of your adventure! Nothing exciting ever happens to me.'

There was a short silence. Turo looked hard at Patch. Was he trying to tell her to forgive Lillian?

'And now it's all gone wrong,' burst out Lillian. 'And those awful people think I really am an heiress and want to kidnap me!'

'And there was I thinking,' said Turo, 'that you really were one of the de Havilands.'

'What do you mean?' asked Patch.

'What, you really ain't heard of 'em?' said Turo.

'They have banks all over the States! They're worth a fortune. If that Reynolds really is the crook you think he is, he must've thought his birthday'd come early when he saw Lillian here all on her lonesome.'

'Oh,' said Lillian and Patch together. They looked at each other. Lillian's eyes were red where she had been crying, and her mouth was pinched into a worried line. Patch tried to imagine what it would feel like to lose someone you love, to have all your hopes dashed and be smuggled onto a boat and have your life turned upside down.

Lillian had lost her Granny. Her sister was all she had left. She had been so desperate to protect Esty, that's why she had said that horrible thing.

Patch thought of all the horrible things she had said when she had been frightened and unhappy. She twiddled the ring, feeling its smooth and sharp contours.

Something shifted.

She reached out and took Lillian's hand. Lillian smiled – a tentative smile. Hoping, but not assuming. Patch squeezed her hand. Made a decision.

'We'll stop them, let them know you're not worth kidnapping,' she said. 'And you're right. We won't tell the captain.'

It was as if the sun had come out. Lillian's tiny smile turned into a blazing grin. She hugged Patch and said 'sorry', and Patch said 'sorry' back and she couldn't believe how good it felt to have Lillian's arms around her and feel her heart beating next to hers.

'So, what's the plan?' said Turo when the hugging had stopped.

Patch picked up one of Lillian's issues of *Girls' Best Friend*.

'Has Lilian de Haviland got any scissors?' she asked.

Lillian rummaged in the trunk and found some tiny nail scissors that matched the brush and mirror set.

Carefully Patch started to cut out letters from the pages. She asked Lillian for soap because there wasn't any glue. After a few minutes of snipping and sticking, she held up the results triumphantly.

'There!'

WE KNOW WHAT YOU ARE PLANNING. DO NOT KIDNAP LILIAN. SHE IS NOT AN HEIRESS. LEAVE US ALONE AND WE WILL LEAVE YOU ALONE TOO.

'You're brilliant, Patch!' said Lillian, relief flooding her features.

'Swell!' said Turo.

'Turo, they're in the regal suite, on the starboard side. Can you post it under the door?' Patch felt giddy with success. Both Lillian and Turo were looking at her like she was the cleverest person in the world.

'I'll do it right now,' he said.

* * *

The next day when Patch woke in her little bunk, a thrill of excitement coursed through her. Today was Friday, her last full day at sea! She had done it. She had survived as a stowaway and a scullion. Lilian was no longer in danger. Tomorrow morning they would dock in New York and they'd go to Tiffany-&-Co-which-looked-like-a-Venetian-palace and they'd ask about the ring. And after that, who knew? She was free to do as she pleased.

The day, as ever, was busy: a whirl of scrubbing, scraping, peeling and chopping. Halfway through the afternoon, Mrs Chilkes called Patch into the pantry. The dumb waiter that served the starboard regal suite had broken, she explained, and she needed someone to carry the tea things up on a tray. All the stewardesses were busy. Young Patchet would have to do.

'You're neat, you're presentable. Tuck your hair behind your ears. Good.'

Patch gulped. Tea to the regal suite. Starboard side. The Reynolds.

Still, they couldn't *do* anything to her. They would've received the note by now and know that Lillian was not an heiress and Patch was no longer a threat. She would just hand over the tea things and go.

'And after you've done that,' called Mrs Chilkes, 'nip down to the stores and fetch me some more eggs.'

Patch took the service lift, which wasn't nearly as fancy as the one by the grand entrance, and emerged onto the promenade deck on the starboard side. It was a cold bright day, the air sharp and salty, the sea swelling gently. Some passengers were relaxing after a late lunch: ladies settling themselves into their steamer chairs, made more comfortable with an array of cushions and travelling rugs; gentlemen strolling and smoking their pipes, pausing to admire the rolling waves.

At the regal suite, she set the tray down on the deck and knocked. After a minute or two the door opened. But it was not Mr Reynolds standing there with his cane and his grey-black curls and his cold sapphire eyes. Nor was it Mrs Reynolds in one of her picture hats, with her breathy voice and habit of clutching her scarves and furs to her throat. It was an elderly gentleman smartly dressed in a grey morning suit.

Startled, she bent to get the tray, and as she did, something caught her eye on the floor. It was her note, pushed under the door by Turo the day before, lying there unnoticed. Quickly, she scooped it up and held it tight in her fist as she passed the tray over.

'At your service Mr . . .?' she said as he took it.

'Sir G Farnham,' he said.

Ask, Patch, ask, she told herself. Sir G was already moving to shut the door.

'Forgive me, Sir G, but I thought Mr and Mrs Reynolds had this suite. Am I mistaken?'

The gentleman regarded Patch curiously. He hadn't expected this little scullion to be so well-spoken.

'My dear child,' he said. 'I have no idea who you mean. My wife and I have been the sole occupants of this suite for the entire journey.' He smiled and gently closed the door. Poor thing, he thought as he took the tea tray through to the parlour. Probably from a fine family but fallen on hard times. Reduced to working as a scullion on a ship. Dreadful, quite dreadful.

On the other side of the door, Patch stood stock

still, her mind working furiously. If this wasn't the Reynoldses' suite then it meant they hadn't got the note. They would still be plotting their dastardly crime. Lillian was still in danger. But where were they?

In a panic, Patch rushed round to the regal suite on the port side and knocked loudly on June's door.

'Why, Patch!' June said when she saw Patch standing there in her new kitchen garb. 'I heard about your fall from grace ... but you're an adaptable girl. I expect you'll manage.' She stepped out from her suite and closed the door behind her. 'Keeping Sid in,' she said by way of explanation. 'He's rather frisky today. Is everything all right?'

'I'm not sure,' said Patch. She shivered. The wind was brisk and her scullion's uniform was thin. 'It's just ... I wanted to ask ... the Reynoldses ... I thought they were occupying the other regal suite?'

'Why on earth do you need to know?' said June.

'Because they're not to be trusted,' said Patch. 'They're up to no good. They want to—' She stopped.

'Want to what?' said June, suddenly alert.

But Patch was already racing away. Eggs. She had to get the eggs for Mrs Chilkes and then she had to find Turo, get him to look at the passenger list that she hoped was still hidden under his bunk, find out where the Reynoldses' cabin was. She shoved the crumpled note into her pocket. There was still time. They could still find the Reynoldses and make them see they were mistaken about Lillian.

* * *

In the cool of the stores on the lower deck, Patch quickly selected two dozen eggs for Mrs Chilkes and piled them into a basket. Closing the door, she hurried back along the passageway towards the stairs that would take her directly to the kitchen on the upper deck and then onwards to find Turo.

She was used to the ship's noises now, the groans and the moans and the constant rumble of the engine. But she didn't see anyone lurking in the shadows, or hear them running after her.

And by the time she realised anything was wrong, it was too late.

Chapter Eighteen

With a sudden force, her pursuer grabbed her from behind, lifted her up by the scruff of her neck and slammed her hard against the wall.

There was a loud crack as Patch's head hit the iron pipes that ran along the length of the corridor. The pain was instant, a kind of searing shriek; she saw an explosion of stars and was dimly aware of dropping the basket, of eggs flying everywhere and the smash of yolk and eggshell splattering the floor. And then there was a struggle, of legs and arms and fists and teeth. Patch fought for all she was worth. But the man was strong. And he had an iron grip.

It was a young man. A handsome man. His hand was

at her throat and his face was pressed up close, inches from hers. There was something familiar about him but she didn't know what. She tried to shout out but his fingers pinched her neck and her jaw and the only thing that came out was a sort of strangled yelp.

The whistle. Scully's whistle. But it was in her pocket and he was strangling her and she could barely breathe.

'Stay out of it,' he hissed. 'Mind yer own business. And if yer don't ... No one will miss ya.' His fingers gripped harder, pressing into her larynx. Her head felt like a balloon about to burst. He was still lifting her up. Her feet kicked uselessly. Her eyes were level with a tiny mole just above his upper lip.

He was choking all the breath out of her. She thought she might die.

A shriek pierced the air and Patch's eyes bulged. For a brief moment she thought the noise had come from her. But then from behind the man she saw a figure rushing towards them, a flying banshee, hair streaming, scarlet slippers pounding. And then the figure was upon them, snarling like a wild animal, wrenching the man off her, screaming at him, pounding him with a stick until he released his grip and staggered off, cursing.

Patch collapsed in a crumpled heap on the floor.

'Patch, are you all right?' It was Babette. She

crouched down next to Patch and pushed her mass of black hair away from her face. It looked like it had been electrified.

'I think so,' whispered Patch sitting up. She blinked hard, trying not to cry.

'What was all that about?'

'Don't know,' spluttered Patch. The man had tried to frighten her and he had succeeded. He had been warning her off. Was it about Lillian? Her throat burned and her head ached. A small part of her was conscious of being disappointed that she had not been able to fight the man herself. She prided herself on her fighting.

Babette stood up and kicked the broken eggs into a small pile with the scarlet tip of her shoe, picked up the basket and disappeared into the stores. When she came back the basket was full of fresh eggs. She sat back down next to Patch and laid a hot hand on her forehead. Her touch seemed to sizzle with something. Strength? Fury? Patch wasn't sure, but it felt good.

'I could see you were about to fight him off,' said Babette, and it was almost like she could read the thoughts in Patch's mind. 'Although you didn't really need me. Anyone can see you're tough as old boots.'

Patch smiled weakly. Tough as old boots. That was

what Meg used to say, all those aeons ago when she had lived with the second-cousin-twice-removed.

'What were you doing down here?' she asked. She saw that the stick Babette had used to beat her attacker with was in fact a wooden ruler.

'Measuring up.'

'For what?'

'We arrive in New York tomorrow so I'll need to get off the ship before we dock. Make my escape!'

'How will you do that?'

'I'll shimmy through there!' Babette indicated a porthole on the other side of the corridor.

The porthole was ironbound, about thirteen inches in diameter. Babette was small, but still.

'Will you fit through it?' asked Patch.

'It's an old trick,' said Babette, 'and people *have* been known to get stuck halfway through, and then they've had to be sawed out.' She stopped, enjoying Patch's horrified expression. 'But not *moi*. I've already arranged for a bucket of grease from Chilkes so I shall slip through like a fish. And on the other side a couple of friendly longshoremen will be waiting to row me across to my next ship!'

She threw back her head and laughed out loud. Tiny gold hoops glinted in her ears.

'You are brave,' said Patch. She had never met anyone as bold and brave before.

'Not always,' said Babette. And for a brief moment a shadow passed over her vivacious features.

She reached out an elegant hand and touched Patch's cheek. It was a kind, thoughtful gesture which had more of an effect on Patch than Babette realised. Patch hadn't experienced many kind, thoughtful touches in her short life.

'Do you ever regret anything?' she asked Babette suddenly. She was thinking about the choices she had made. Running away, getting on this ship. Going to New York. She had yearned for adventure. But she hadn't expected to get tangled up in things she didn't understand. She rubbed her throat where it still felt sore. She hadn't expected such real-life danger.

Something flickered at the edges of Babette's eyes.

'Do I regret anything? My itchy feet,' she said, ruefully. 'If you have to keep moving, you have to relinquish some things. I tried to settle down once, and I couldn't do it.'

Was her lip trembling? As if she might cry? Patch wasn't sure. But now Babette was moving away, busying herself with winding her hair on top of her head and securing it with the ruler. She turned to Patch and her face was full of concern.

'But Patch, really, who *was* that? I feel I have seen him somewhere before but I can't place him.'

'Me too,' said Patch. Babette was right. There was something about him that had been uncannily familiar.

* * *

It wasn't until the pair had parted ways that Patch put her hand to her throat and realised something was missing.

The ribbon was still there. But not the ring.

He must have taken it!

The handsome face thrust up close to hers.

His breath hot on her cheek.

The mole just above his upper lip.

The mole!

The thought hit Patch like a thunderbolt. It was in exactly the same place as Mrs Reynolds's beauty spot.

Surely not?

Patch stopped short. Trying to make sense of this preposterous fact.

Either Mrs Reynolds had an identical male twin. Or she was a he – in disguise.

Patch's mind whirred and whirled. The picture hat. The breathy voice. The scarves and the furs at her or his throat.

If Mrs Reynolds was really a Mr, then could it have been him with the other Mr Reynolds that she had overheard when she'd been hiding in the lifeboat? He had the same rough voice. He'd called her a whiny brat. He'd thought she, Patch, might muck up their plan.

Patch dumped the eggs and tore down the corridor. Mrs Chilkes would have to wait. Lillian couldn't.

But when she reached the cabin, instead of Lillian, she found Esty hovering in the doorway.

'Oh!' said Patch. The cabin was still in a state, the trunk gaping open, the contents strewn all over the floor. Where was Lillian? Was she too late?

No time to tell Esty she knew she was Lillian's sister or explain about her scullion's outfit.

'Where is she?' she burst out.

'She had an invitation to tea with Mrs Fortune in the regal suite,' said Esty, a frown creasing her brow. 'She took your roller skates. I expected her to be back down here for her dinner. It's unusual for her to be gone so long. To tell you the truth, I'm a little worried.'

* * *

Patch was racing along the promenade deck when she ran full pelt into Turo. He staggered back, dropping the huge pile of newspapers he was carrying. They landed with a loud slap, scattering all across the deck and flapping in the breeze.

'Sorry!' said Patch. 'I didn't mean to, it's just . . .'

In a torrent she told him about the regal suite. And the attack.

'They didn't get the note. We need to find out where their cabin is . . . and find Lillian too. I think she's safe with June for the time being. I'm on my way there now.'

The wind had picked up and the newspapers began to flutter across the deck like angry birds. One flew up and hit her, thwack, in the face. She grabbed it, batted it straight and was just about to hand it back to Turo when something caught her eye.

Patch gripped the page and stared.

Halfway down was a large photograph. It was terribly smudged, but Patch could just about make out that it was taken in the style of an old-fashioned family portrait, with two figures standing stiffly behind a seated one. Only one of the standing figures was clear enough to examine closely. Patch bashed the paper straight and brought it close. It was a man, a young man. And there was something recognisable about him. She drew a shocked breath. Could it really be . . .

It was!

Her hand rushed to her throat. She could see the mole! It was him. The handsome young man who had just attacked her.

Her eyes shot up to the headline.

The air on deck seemed to turn a degree or two colder.

She dropped to her knees and with a terrible sense of foreboding, began to read:

WANTED FOR MURDER – REWARD OFFERED

Yesterday Scotland Yard announced a nationwide manhunt for one of the most notorious criminal families in the British Isles. Believed to operate under a variety of names, but chiefly known as the Snells, they head up an infamous London-based gang known as The Fifty Elephants. The gang routinely terrorise shoppers in the West End, running amok and regularly plundering fashion and jewellery shops. A fortnight ago they masterminded a simultaneous raid on ten jewellery shops, making away with thousands of pounds' worth of loose diamonds.

The family are highly skilled at covering their tracks, but after numerous failed investigations, the police have finally made a breakthrough. The gentleman in charge of the investigation, Inspector Grave, has iron-clad evidence linking them to the murder of a London constable earlier this month.

'The public are asked to be alert,' said Inspector Grave. 'The Snells are skilled con artists. Frank Junior in particular has a talent for disguise. In the past he has posed as a schoolboy, a chimney sweep, a curate and a lady detective. Mrs Snell has been known to infiltrate all levels of society owing to her fabled charm. Frank Senior is to be avoided at all costs. He is a brute, plain and simple. Be on your guard. All three are wily opportunists, extremely violent and capable of murder.'

The public are asked to report any sightings of the family to the police. Rumours that they have been hiding in Liverpool have not been substantiated. A generous reward is offered.

Chapter Nineteen

P atch staggered to her feet. The wind plucked at the newspaper but she held on to it fast.

'It's Mr and Mrs Reynolds!' said Patch. Her heart was hammering so hard it felt like it might explode. 'The Snells: Frank Junior and Frank Senior.' The article had specifically said he had a talent for disguise. It must've been an effort pretending to be a lady all this time. No wonder she— *he'd* had a 'headache' yesterday.

'Notorious! Violent!' said Turo, hugging the wad of newspapers to his chest as if for protection. 'We've got to get to Lillian before they do! When they find out she's not who they think she is, they're gonna get angry and who knows what they might do ...'

'Oh don't!' cried Patch, although he was only voicing exactly what she had already thought. The realisation was shocking, sending icy shivers of fear skittering up her spine.

'You can't mess with these types, Patch! When you've found Lillian you've *gotta* go see the captain,' said Turo. 'He needs to know.'

'But Esty and Matty...'

'Holy moly, this is acres bigger than that, Patch! Esty and Matty getting found out is small fry compared to ... murder.'

'You're right. I'll get Lillian and meet you ...'

'In the hold, where you found Babette,' said Turo. 'We can hide her there, keep her out of their clutches.'

'And then we'll go together to the captain and tell him everything. Keep this safe.' She tore the page out of the newspaper and handed it over. 'When he sees it, he'll have to listen to us.'

* * *

The promenade deck was empty now. Everyone was at dinner. But further along Patch could see the lights to the regal suite blazing. Please let June still be there! And please let Lillian be safe!

Patch only had to bash on the regal suite door once before June appeared, resplendent in a peacock blue dress with a waterfall of crimson lace at the collar.

'Oh, thank *goodness* you're not at dinner,' Patch burst out. She peered behind June into the parlour. Her heart dipped. 'Is Lillian not with you?'

'You'd better come in,' June stood back.

'Not if she isn't here,' said Patch. 'I need to find her now, it's urgent.'

'Come in, Patch, do,' said June more firmly. She took Patch's hand and gently nudged her in, kicking the door shut behind her.

'Who is it, Old Ma?'

Patch froze.

The voice floating in from one of the adjacent rooms was dreadfully familiar.

She removed her hand from June's. Blood began to pound in her ears; her skin seemed to buzz as if every nerve in her body had become electrified.

'Who ... is that ...?'

She noticed that June wasn't smiling any more. Her gold tooth glinted in a way that suddenly seemed rather ominous. On her little finger was a ring.

Patch's ring.

'You don't need to worry about Lillian. She is quite

safe.' Her voice had taken on a steely quality. The laughter, the lightness, had disappeared.

Patch felt as though she had been knocked sideways.

The photograph in the paper had *three* people in it. There had been two men. Father and son. But there had been a woman as well. A woman of 'fabled charm'.

Could that woman really be June?

Patch felt a dull red fury flood her veins.

She had been tricked.

'Where's Lillian?' she demanded.

June smiled. Removed her spectacles. And Patch saw that her eyes were the colour of cold, hard sapphires. Exactly the same as Mr Reynolds.

On the sofa something twitched and Patch became aware of a pair of feet, clad in black patent-leather shoes, crossed at the ankle. The figure sat up. Identical bright blue eyes, black-grey curls.

'Now you've disturbed Frank,' said June.

'Old Ma!' called the voice again.

'In a minute!' yelled June.

'Well. Look what the cat dragged in,' whispered Mr Reynolds-now-Frank Senior. He was staring at Patch in a way that made her skin crawl. A brute, the newspaper had said. Plain and simple.

'Come to meddle 'ave ya?' His voice was quiet yet full

of menace. Not the debonair gentleman now. More like an evil Bill Sikes.

'Not got the message yet? Don't tell me Frank Junior didn't put the fear of God into you? Looks like we might have to shut you up once an' for all . . .'

'Where's Lillian?' Patch repeated. She tried to keep the panic out of her voice, but it was hard. Frank Senior was frightening. A nerve twitched frantically under his eye. He cracked his ring-crammed knuckles.

A flurry of movement and Sid scampered into the room. He looked from June to Patch and back to June again. Immediately Patch could see he knew that something was wrong. He flattened his ears and uttered a long, low whine.

'And you can stay out of it,' muttered Frank Senior to the dog. 'Ma, pass me my cane.'

Sid ducked his head and backed away from Frank Senior. He came close to Patch, leaning his hard little body against her legs. She could feel him trembling.

Babette *had* been right. He *was* scared of June. Goodness knows how she treated him when no one was looking. All those times he'd found Patch or followed her. He'd been trying to run away from his owner. And what had Patch done? She had taken him straight back home.

From the room next door came a loud thud, followed by a scuffling noise and then a bang as though a cupboard door had been slammed shut.

'Lillian *is* here, isn't she?' said Patch. 'What have you done to her? Lillian! Don't worry, I'm here!'

'Shut your gob!' said Frank Senior threateningly. He took a step towards her. 'Ma, I said I want my cane!'

'I heard you, my dear, but where is it?'

'You don't understand,' said Patch quickly. 'She's not who you think she is . . .'

In an instant Frank Senior was upon her, twisting her arms behind her back with such strength they burned.

'I said shut it and I mean shut it. Ma, forget the cane and open the trunk.'

In a terrible rush, Patch remembered the night when she'd been crouched in the lifeboat. What had he said? 'She gets in the way, she's out of the picture. No one's gonna notice a disappeared kid.'

'No, you need to listen to me!' she was shouting now. She had to make them understand their mistake.

Another thump came from the room next door. The sound of Frank Junior swearing.

'Lillian, are you there?' yelled Patch. But now Frank Senior was holding her in his vice-like grip and June was binding a bandage round her mouth and it was so tight she could barely breathe, let alone cry out.

'Frank saw you hiding in that lifeboat. We guessed you dodged your way on board. Not a soul in the world will miss you. No one will be any the wiser if you disappear,' said June.

Patch blinked back a tear. The gag was cutting into her mouth. *Not a soul in the world.* Was that true? Turo would miss her. Lillian would too. Even Babette and Mrs Chilkes might wonder where she was. She watched, powerless as June unlocked and opened a large metal trunk. The lid creaked. Patch made her body go stiff and heavy so that Frank Senior had to drag her towards it like a leaden log.

There was a bark and a sudden movement of muscled body and bared teeth. Sid! He would miss her! And she would miss him.

'Get back, dog,' shrieked June.

'Ouch!' Frank Senior cried out and let go of Patch. 'Ma, he blinkin' bit me!'

Sid growled. He bared his teeth again, showing a set of knife-sharp incisors, and went for Frank once more. Frank leapt away, howling.

'Ma, control the brute! What's the point of keepin' a fightin' dog if it goes for the wrong person? If you'd only got my cane when I asked for it!' He collapsed on the sofa, gripping his leg. A trickle of blood sploshed onto the rug leaving a poppy-shaped stain.

'Dog!' screeched June. But now Sid was going for her, snarling ferociously, locking his jaws round her ankle, making her writhe and kick out at him but he wouldn't let go.

'She's a little animal, that one.'

It was Frank Junior, standing in the doorway. Was he talking about Lillian? His nose looked crooked and a violet-black bruise glowered under one eye. His gaze took in Frank Senior nursing his leg on the sofa and June thrashing about with Sid.

'What's goin' on?'

'Don't just stand there,' screamed June. 'Get the dog off me!'

As Frank Junior went to his Old Ma, in a flash Patch turned and made a dash for the door. Out of the cabin, onto the dark deck. She stopped, disorientated. Where was the sky? Where was the sea? She couldn't see anything! No moon. No stars. The whole world was shrouded in a thick, black, swirling fog.

Behind her she heard the door slam. They were coming. She had to get away. She had to get to the captain, get help quick.

With a giant spurt she launched herself into the blackness and began running blind, the only sounds the roar and roil of the sea and the ragged gasp of her breath.

A blood-curdling yell and then the pounding of dreaded footsteps, tearing after her, chasing her, hunting her down. Was it Frank Junior? Probably. And what would he do when he caught her? Toss her overboard? No one was about. No one would see.

She was all alone on this enormous ship, a mouse to his cat.

A great sob fought its way up to her throat and then she heard something else, something scampering along beside her, the click of claws on the wooden deck.

'Oh Sid, Sid,' she cried, except no sound came out because the bandages were tied so tight and her words were muffled.

On she ran, all the way along the promenade deck, trusting her feet instead of her sight, dipping in and out of shelters, weaving her way past the towering funnels and crashing into the grand entrance. The blaze of light was so sudden it made her squint. Quick, quick, up the deserted staircase, ignoring the painful burning in her chest, tripping over her feet, bursting through the doors to the boat deck, back out into the cold night air.

He was still following, and he was closer now, because she could hear him swearing and panting. Please, please, she must be nearly there! And then there it was! A glimmering light and the steps up to the bridge, looming out of the fog. Could she make it? She might. She tried to cry out but the bandage prevented her. She tore at it, desperately trying to yank it off, taking the steps two at a time, and still the gag was stopping her voice and—

'Got yer.'

One powerful grab was all it took, and now he was wrenching her into the shadows and she could see the dim glow of the lights in the wheelhouse but they couldn't see her, and they couldn't hear her either.

'Old Ma said to push you overboard and that's exactly what I'm going to do,' he muttered. And then he was lifting her up and for a brief moment there was a silent struggle, and she was resisting, resisting, scrabbling and clawing, but it was no good because he gave her one last violent shove and then she was flying into nothingness, tumbling through the air towards the smack of the sea and the roar of the waves that would surely swallow her up.

Chapter Twenty

Patch landed with a terrible thud.

For a split second she felt nothing. Then pain bloomed, spreading all the way up her body to her head. She raised her hand to her scalp and felt something sticky. Her legs and arms were all cricked up in a tangle of rope, rope that was so thick and scratchy it tore at her skin.

Every bone in her body seemed to be screaming.

But it didn't matter. It didn't matter because she hadn't been swallowed up by the sea. She hadn't drowned!

With an effort she raised her throbbing head to get her bearings, and as her eyes adjusted to the dark, she began to make out shapes in the foggy gloom, shapes that belonged to the mechanics of the ship, and a mass of giant cables.

The wind whistled, the boat thrummed, but otherwise there were no other noises. Not a scamper or a snuffle could be heard.

Please let Sid not be in the sea!

Something rustled. Was *that* Sid? Hope sparked. But no. It was footsteps. Human ones. Light, not heavy. The swish of a skirt.

Patch shrank back. Could it be June? Come to finish the job and push her properly overboard? She tried to move, to drag herself into a hiding place. But it was too late. Whoever it was had already found her. A hot hand rested on her forehead.

'Who did this to you!'

It was Babette dressed in her third-class costume, the soft material of her patched shawl brushing against Patch's cheek. Relief swept over Patch.

Not June.

Patch tried to explain. But the gag was still on.

'Ssshh, let's get you inside.'

Babette wrapped her wiry arms around Patch and half carried, half dragged her over the rope, past a giant anchor and down a flight of steps, bump, bump, bump, setting her down as gently as she could in a dark corner by a doorway. Deftly she untied the gag and Patch let out a long shuddery gasp. She had never been so pleased to see anyone in her entire life.

'Why aren't I in the sea? Where am I?'

'You fell from the bridge and landed on the foredeck. What were you doing up there?'

'I didn't fall, I was pushed!' said Patch. Her voice was hoarse. 'They meant me to drown. They want to disappear me.'

Babette jerked back and then she did something that Patch didn't understand. She cupped her hands over her mouth and hollered 'Girl overboard,' three times, high and wild and clear.

And immediately Patch heard other shouts, and whistles and a big boom splitting the air.

'That should do it,' said Babette. 'Whoever wants you dead will think you *are* dead. Now come.' And she kicked open the door which was marked Third Class and pulled Patch through.

'Can you walk? Stand up, let's test your bones.'

Patch stood and miraculously everything did seem to work, even if her nuts and bolts were a bit rusty. And then Babette was grabbing her and saying, 'Time to hide,' and they were stumbling, hurrying, along passageway after passageway, down another flight of steps, past the third-class ladies room, past the dining room and down again to the lower deck and the rumble of the engines.

Quick, quick, they rushed along, past endless cabins all squeezed together, towards the heat and the noise of the bunkers and the boiler rooms, and then on to the storerooms and, finally, to a door labelled Mail Room.

'At last,' said Babette, leading the way. And Patch saw that she had made herself a sort of nest hidden away behind a wall of mail sacks.

She had spread out several eiderdowns that looked suspiciously like the ones that were in Lillian's cabin, and there were blankets too, and pillows. Babette gestured for Patch to sit down and then, from that bottomless bag of hers, fished out a kettle and two cups.

'Tea?' she said. 'You look like you could use it,' and she swept off. Patch sat in a daze, still in shock, trying to work things out, but her head hurt and her mind felt battered and after a while she gave up. Then Babette was back with two cups of steaming tea and she propped Patch up against the pillows and covered her with blankets.

'I don't understand why I'm not drowndead,' said Patch. She said it like Mr Peggotty in *David Copperfield*.

She must be a bit delirious. The tea was hot and deliciously sweet. The warmth of it seemed to trickle all the way down to her toes. 'He pushed me.'

'Whoever this *he* is, he's stupid,' said Babette. 'If you want to push someone overboard, you do it on the starboard side or port, not from the bridge!'

Patch sat quietly for a bit while Babette dipped a cloth in warm water and dabbed at the sore bit on her head.

'Ouch,' said Babette sympathetically. 'But it looks worse than it is. You'll live.'

All of a sudden Patch spat out a mouthful of hot tea. 'Lillian! They've got her! We have to—'

'I think it's time to tell me,' said Babette firmly, settling herself against the pillows next to Patch, 'who *they* are.'

So Patch told her about the Snells, and about how bad they were, and how they had captured Lillian because they thought she was an heiress, worth incredible riches, and how she was in the gravest danger.

'I knew it!' said Babette when Patch had finished, slapping her head with her hand. 'I knew there was something not at all right about that Fortune woman ...'

'We've got to go back up there and rescue Lillian!'

said Patch. 'I was on my way to the captain and that's when ...'

She slumped back down. She felt dizzy. The room had started to swim.

'Ssssh,' said Babette. 'You've bought yourself some time. The ship will be in uproar thinking someone has gone overboard. The Snells will think you are out of the picture. They won't do anything to Lillian yet. As far as they are concerned, she is still their prize bounty.'

The room dimmed and Patch shut her eyes. She remembered the thudding noises and the sound of something slamming shut. Had Frank Junior locked Lillian inside a cupboard? Was she all squished up in the dark? Frightened for her life?

She must've put up a fight though. Frank Junior's smashed nose and black eye were proof of that. Patch sat up again and the room tilted alarmingly.

'But I have to get to Turo. He's waiting for me in the hold.'

'Just a little rest first,' said Babette soothingly. And she began to sing a beautiful, melodious song, full of yearning for waves and water, a song that reminded Patch of something – she didn't know what – that went way, way back, aeons before this journey had started, something long forgotten but determined to find her curled up in this nest of eiderdowns deep beneath the sea.

* * *

It was pitch black when Patch awoke. For a minute she struggled to remember where she was. Then she felt a dull throb in her scalp and heard the regular sound of someone breathing next to her. In a rush, everything came flooding back.

The Snells.

Lillian locked up.

Turo waiting.

Quiet as a mouse, Patch crept out of the makeshift bed and crawled across the room, her eyes fixed on the chink of light that was coming from under the door. Gingerly she rose to her feet and for a split second her head objected and the room tilted, but somehow she stayed upright. Then, when she had regained her balance, she slipped out into the corridor.

Past the storerooms, past the boiler rooms, past the endless cabins all squished up together. It didn't take long to run back along the length of the boat and there it was, the crew's quarters.

No one was about. It was the dead of night. She clambered down the almost vertical steps to the hold.

'*Madonna mia*! You're alive!' said Turo.

He was lying on the lion's back, his arms entwined in its mane, the menagerie of animals looming in the gloom behind him. They seemed to be glaring at her, just like he was. Patch took a step closer. His eyes were red.

'Mrs Chilkes was goin' crazy! "Girl overboard," we heard, and you were nowhere to be found! We thought . . .' He rubbed his face with his fists. 'I tried to get to the captain but I couldn't get near him. No one listens to the boots.'

'I'm not dead but I nearly was,' said Patch, collapsing against the leopard. 'June's in on it too, Turo. They're all from the same family. Grandmother, father and son. And they've already got Lillian.'

She related the events of the past few hours. 'Sid was with me on deck when Frank Junior was chasing me but when I fell, I don't know what happened to him . . .'

'Woah!' said Turo. 'Whaddaya waiting for? Let's go see the captain right now.'

'No,' said Patch.

'Whaddaya mean, no?' Turo was looking at her

aghast. 'They tried to *kill* ya, Patch. Lillian might already *be* dead.'

'She won't be. They still think she is a de Haviland,' she said. 'She's still their prize.'

'If you don't wanna go see the captain, what *do* you wanna do?'

Patch thought about all the daredevil adventures she had read about in her *Girls' Best Friend* comics. The heroines who always solved the most dreadful problems themselves.

'The Snells are bound to be planning to smuggle Lillian off the ship somehow, and when they're on dry land I should think they'll demand a ransom,' she said. 'But now we know what they're up to, what's to stop us catching them ourselves?'

'And win the reward d'you mean?' said Turo, his eyes brightening.

'Everyone will be so pleased with us and we'll get our pictures in the papers, and the captain will have to be gracious and let Esty and Matty keep their jobs!'

'But how . . .' said Turo.

They both went quiet.

'What's that?'

There was a clatter and the murmur of voices. A head appeared in the opening of the hatch, a pale face surrounded by a cloud of raven black hair. Babette. And behind her jostled Jimmy carrying his trombone, and there was Esty, her face streaked with tears.

'I knew you'd be here!' Babette announced, jumping down, not even bothering with the ladder, and landing with the grace of a cat.

'Will you look at that!' said Jimmy, leaping down after her and taking in the menagerie of animals.

Esty was the last down. She peered around hopefully, as though Lillian might appear at any second. 'Babette insists she's not gone overboard,' Esty said to Patch, 'but if that's true, then where is she?'

'With the Reynoldses who are really the Snells,' said Patch. She stepped forward and hugged Esty. 'But we're going to get her back.'

Chapter Twenty-One

'We'll have to act quickly,' said Babette. 'Whatever your plan is, Patch, it'll be easier to carry out under cover of darkness. It'll be dawn in under an hour.'

Patch coughed twice and felt for the ring that wasn't there. *What was the plan?*

'Babette's right,' said Jimmy. 'Once we've passed the lightship *Ambrose*, there's only another twenty miles until we dock.'

Twenty miles. Patch had to think of something fast, or risk losing Lillian forever.

'Well strike me down!' Jimmy had turned his attention away from Patch and was looking with renewed interest at the menagerie of animals. He stepped over to the zebra and examined the label clipped to its ear. 'These must be the first of Arkley's animals! I heard he was collecting specimens for a new exhibit at the museum, and here they are!' He disappeared from view as he made his way deeper into the hold.

'Oh, what does it matter about the animals?' cried Esty. 'It's Lillian we have to think about. I don't know why you brought me here,' she said to Babette, starting to climb back up the ladder. 'It's obvious Patch doesn't have a plan. I'm going to wake Matty and then we'll go to the captain together. We'll come clean, admit everything and … What's that?' She stopped, her eyes wide.

Ear-splitting booming sounds were filling the hold, like a herd of trumpeting elephants followed by an unearthly growling.

'Holy moly!' gasped Turo. It was as if the animals had somehow come to life. Very carefully he slid off the lion, his eyes wide.

'Fooled ya!' Jimmy cried, reappearing from behind the leopard. He was laughing and they all saw that the noises had come not from the animals but from his trombone.

Patch looked from the animals, to Jimmy, to the trombone.

'I've got it!' she said. And then she said it louder because no one was listening.

'I've got it! I've got a plan!'

* * *

Without the hustle and bustle and the spitting pots and pans, in the very early hours of the morning the kitchen was like another world; a ghost kitchen, thought Patch as she followed Esty between the towering ovens to the two little cupboards several feet apart from each other. One had the letter S above it for starboard and the other had the letter P for port.

'That's it,' said Esty, pointing at the one that read P. The cupboard had two doors covered in wire mesh. It was positioned at shoulder height and not much bigger than a large tea tray.

Patch looked at the dumb waiter doubtfully. It had seemed like such a good idea when it had popped into her head in the hold. The perfect way to carry her up into the heart of the regal suite.

But she wasn't at all sure that she would fit inside.

To the right of the cupboard was a polished wooden

handle. The handle that would operate the pulley and that Esty – Patch darted a glance at her slight frame – would have to use all her strength to turn.

'No need to look so worried,' said Esty. 'Granny always said I had the strength of a horse.'

She fished something out of her pocket and passed it to Patch. 'You'll need this.' It was a large key, exactly like the one Lillian had shown Patch a few days before. 'It's a master key. It'll get you in anywhere, including cupboards and wardrobes. If Lillian's locked up, this'll get her out.'

'But Lillian's already got one . . .' started Patch, and it suddenly struck her that if that was the case, why hadn't she already used it to rescue herself?

Esty's eyes met Patch's. 'She did have one,' she said miserably. 'I confiscated it yesterday because I was sick of the tales she was telling. Oh, this is all my fault . . .'

'Esty,' said Patch, laying a hand on her arm. 'It's going to be all right. I promise.'

'I do hope so!' said Esty with a sniff. 'Come on, let's get you in.'

Somehow Patch squished herself into the tiny space, her knees and neck and elbows all bent into the most unusual angles.

'Oh!' said Esty as a thought struck her, 'with no

lights an' all, you'd better take these.' She tossed Patch a box of matches, nodded a quick goodbye, and flipped the doors shut.

The dumb waiter smelled of burnt toast and boiled egg, and it wasn't used to carrying anything half as heavy as Patch. No wonder the pulleys and weights squeaked a chorus of complaints as the little lift ascended, inch by painful inch.

At last the contraption shuddered to a halt and the squeaking ceased. On the other side of the door lay the regal suite's master bedroom – and the Snells. The sound of a long wheezy snore floated through the wire mesh of the doors – so close it felt as if June was actually in the dumb waiter with Patch.

She shivered.

Hopefully, Babette had done what she had said she would – creep into the fuse room and turn the electricity off.

Hopefully, Jimmy, Matty and Turo were in place.

And then quite distinctly she heard it. A long, low growl.

The plan had started.

On the other side of the little door came a snuffle and then a phlegmy cough. At the same time, the growling increased in volume until it became a rumble, and the rumble grew until it matched the vibration of the ship, and all around the air seemed to tremble. Patch balled her hands into fists and held her breath.

She could hear June lurching blindly round the cabin. Trying in vain to turn the lights on. And then the sound of elephants trumpeting. In the dark, Patch couldn't help smiling. Jimmy really was a genius.

'Frank Junior?'

'Old Ma?'

Patch put her ear to the little door. She could hear scrambling and then, 'Frank, what in hellfire is that noise? And why aren't the lights working?'

More crashing, more stumbling. Dreadful-sounding words that Patch had never heard before.

'Old Ma, get out here!'

The slam of a door.

Quick. Patch was out of the dumb waiter, tumbling hard into the pitch black of June's bedroom. Ouch. A searing pain in her shoulder. Mustn't worry about that now.

'Lillian,' she hissed. 'Are you in here?'

Nothing. And she couldn't see anything either.

From the direction of the parlour she could hear screams and a lot of clanking and smashing.

Something rustled. 'Lillian?'

A sad-sounding whine.

It was coming from under the bed.

'Sid!'

Patch knelt down, fumbled for the matches in her pocket and struck one. The flame flickered blueyorange, casting a weak light on the quivering dog, a muzzle over its mouth, his hind leg tied to the bed with a spotted silk scarf.

'Oh, Sid they *have* mistreated you!' she cried. The match burned out and Patch wriggled under the bed, feeling for the dog, tearing the muzzle off and untying his leg. He butted his egg-head against her gratefully, his warm body trembling against hers.

'Sid, where's Lillian? Show me.' And in the dark she crawled after the dog, following his snuffles and snorts out of the room, along the hall and into the adjacent room. He gave a quiet yelp.

She struck another match. The dog was on his hind legs, scrabbling at the door of a wardrobe. Something thudded. Almost imperceptibly the wardrobe shuddered.

Lillian!

Faster, faster, get the key in the lock. But now the match had been snuffed out, Patch couldn't locate the keyhole. She stabbed ineffectually at the door while the thumping inside got more and more agitated and Sid's whines grew louder and louder and then yes! The key slipped in, turned smoothly and . . .

Out whooshed Lillian, roller skates and all, and for one brief, hilarious moment, the dog and the girls were caught in a tangle of arms and skates and furiously wagging tail, and although they couldn't see each other, they could feel each other, and the relief was so great that Patch had to clamp her hand over her mouth to stop the laughter spurting out.

And then the lights flashed on and the girls blinked at each other, and grasping hands, they rushed into the parlour, Sid at their heels.

Chairs had been upturned, a glass decanter smashed to smithereens, the painting of the Italianate villa had dropped from the wall to the floor. Something tickled Patch's ankle. She looked down and screamed. June's *head*? And then she saw it was only hair, a wig in fact, of silvery platinum curls.

She plucked it up, and as she did, a cry of utter fury ripped through the air.

Backed into a corner were Frank Junior, wild-eyed in his nightshirt, and June, almost unrecognisable with her head of close-cropped, gunmetal-grey hair.

Towering over them were Turo wielding a mop like

a sword, Matty brandishing a rolling pin, and Jimmy armed with a silver candlestick in one hand and his trombone in the other.

'Drop that!' hissed June at Patch.

Patch turned the wig over in her hands. The inside was fashioned out of calfskin. But it wasn't smooth. She could feel something nobbly under the surface, like gravel, or tiny stones.

'Frank?' June turned to her grandson who quailed under her piercing gaze. 'I thought you said the job was done?'

'It *was*, Old Ma!' Frank Junior was looking at Patch as though she were a ghost stepped straight out of a penny dreadful.

But Patch had stopped listening. Instead she was ripping open the wig and watching as dozens of glittering stones scattered all over the floor.

'Diamonds!' breathed Turo.

Patch stepped towards June. 'Give me my ring,' she demanded.

June slid the ring off her little finger and handed it over, scowling. Patch slipped it onto her thumb.

The door crashed open and Esty burst in.

'Lil!' she cried, rushing over to catch her sister in a fierce hug.

'I tried to tell you that Lillian isn't who you think she is, but you wouldn't listen!' said Patch, addressing June. 'She's *not* an heiress! She *doesn't* live in a house on Fifth Avenue and there *is* no Mr and Mrs de Haviland. Are you listening now?'

'But Patch . . .' started Turo.

Patch waved a hand at him. She was enjoying this. It was like the final act of a play and she was the star.

'But of course, you're *not* June Fortune, are you? You're Mrs Snell. Wanted for theft' – she pointed a toe at the precious stones winking and blinking on the floor – 'and murder by Scotland Yard. Did you know, rather a large reward's been offered for your capture?'

'Patch, listen!' shouted Turo.

'What? What's the matter?' He was jumping up and down as if an army of biting ants were attacking his ankles.

'Where's Frank Senior?' he said.

Patch looked all around the room. Where *was* he?

'Ha!' said June. And even though she was crouched on the floor, wigless and with her nightgown on, she still looked formidable. A diabolical smile stretched across her face.

'And there was I, thinking you'd never ask.'

Chapter Twenty-Two

A grey light seeped through a gap in the curtains. Dawn had come already. An urgent drum began to beat a steady rhythm deep in Patch's chest.

'Tie them up,' she commanded.

They waited while Esty and Matty relieved the damask curtains of their heavy cord ties, and used the rope to bind the pair's hands and feet.

'It won't do any good,' said June.

'It better had,' retorted Patch. 'Now tell us. Where *is* Frank Senior?'

'Wouldn't you like to know!'

Turo raised his mop threateningly over Frank Junior's head. A few drops of dirty grey liquid sploshed onto him and he shook his head furiously, like a wet dog.

'Come on!' said Patch. 'Tell us or else . . .'

'Go on, Old Ma,' whined Frank Junior.

June rolled her eyes and sighed. 'The truth of it is, you're too late. At this very moment my Frank is . . . making friends, shall we say, with the captain.'

'Making friends?' echoed Patch.

'In a manner of speaking, yes,' said June.

Patch turned to the others. 'We need to get up to the bridge as quick as we can.'

* * *

Outside, fingers of yellowy-pink slanted through grey clouds, gulls circled noisily overhead, and in the distance a mass of tall buildings jutted up into the morning sky.

The ship boomed proudly. All around, tugboats, wreathed in puffs of smoke, dotted the silvery sea. Passengers were beginning to throng the deck, jostling for position. Everyone wanted to claim the best view of the city as the ship sailed into port.

But views were the last thing Patch and her friends had on their minds. Instead, they had their heads down and their elbows out, barging their way through the growing crowds.

To the observer, they were a curious group. In the lead was a determined-looking scullion; next was a gangly ship hand, and after him, an old-fashioned girl staggering along on roller skates; and just behind them was a copper-headed steward with the brilliant Jimmy Taylor and a trussed-up couple, swearing so profusely some people had to cover their ears. Bringing up the rear, was a square-snouted dog, and there was that nice stewardess, the one who could always be relied upon, who waited on the very best families in first class.

No one noticed the figure dressed in third-class rags darting in the shadows, almost invisible apart from her scarlet shoes.

The procession hurried along the promenade deck, ducked into the grand entrance, straggled past the palms, clomped up the stairs and bashed through the doors back out onto the boat deck.

Not for them the views of New York City. Not for them to stand and stare at the magnificent statue of a woman holding a torch high towards the sky, nor at the distant bridge spanning the expanse of water where the sea became a river.

No. On they went, chests thumping, hearts

pounding, tripping over one another, scrambling up the steps that led to the bridge.

Just as June had predicted, there was Frank Senior huddled suspiciously close to the bulk of the captain.

'Don't listen to him!' yelled Patch.

'Step away!' shouted Lillian. She stamped her foot like an angry bull and the wheels of her skates whirred menacingly.

The men turned. Frank's eyes narrowed. He gripped his silver-topped cane and his rings flashed in the early morning sun.

'How in hell did you get out?' he demanded of Lillian. And then, looking at Patch in amazement, he exclaimed, 'You're meant to be dead!'

'Frank! She isn't who we thought she was!' Mrs Snell and Frank Junior stumbled up the stairs with Matty and Jimmy.

'Ma!' Snell's sapphire-blue eyes burned.

'What in God's name is going on?' The captain looked from the children to Frank Snell and back again. He was a large fellow, quite splendid in his uniform. His big puffed-up chest quivered.

Sid echoed the captain's question with a short, sharp bark.

'Whatever he's told you, it's a lie!' shouted Lillian.

'Show the captain the newspaper, Turo,' said Patch.

But Frank was doing something with his cane. A flick of the wrist, a twirl of the stick, and from the bottom a deadly-looking steel blade shot out, which he pointed at the Captain's chest.

'Not one step further,' he hissed at the children. 'Or I'll skewer the captain good and proper. Captain? If you don't make a fuss, then everything will be just fine.'

Beneath his beard and whiskers, the captain paled. He drew in a sharp breath. 'You don't want to be doing this, my man. Now come on, let's sort this out like gentlemen.'

'Gentlemen?' scoffed Frank Senior. 'That may apply to you. Not I.' He looked, Patch thought, like the devil.

'Now listen carefully,' he said all soft and insinuating. 'It's quite simple. I want you to take me, my ma and my son out in one of them lifeboats. Drop us off further down the coast. Not too much to ask is it? Do what I say and you'll come to no harm.'

The captain seemed to shrink. Snell nudged the tip of the blade against his chest, which was no longer puffed up and proud. The blade made a little indentation next to the shiny gold buttons.

'Stop!' Patch cried. What could she do? She turned to Turo and Lillian but they were looking as frightened as she felt. Could they all just jump on Snell? Try to overpower him? But what if the shock of it caused the blade to plunge deep into the captain's chest?

'Come on man, move!' said Snell impatiently.

Patch could see uncertainty flickering in the captain's eyes. And then she remembered.

Scully. The stokers.

What had he said? If she ever needed help, she must whistle.

Frantically she pulled the whistle out of her pocket, raised it to her lips and blew. The shrill whistle rang out, once, twice.

Despite the thrum of the engines, Patch could hear an identical whistle on the deck below. And further away, another one, on the deck below that. And then another and another. She had started a chain of whistles! A thrill swept through her as she pictured the whistles descending all the way down, down, into the very bowels of the boat.

For the first time in days, the constant vibrations of the ship juddered to a halt; the only sounds were the distant chatter of the passengers and the buffeting wind between the rigging and masts.

The engines had cut out!

'What have you done?' shouted Frank threateningly. 'Give that here!' He reached out for the whistle with one hand, prodding the captain's jacket with the blade in the other. 'Shut up with your whistling! Why has the ship stopped?'

Patch stepped back, taking the whistle with her. Snell's gaze was murderous. Oh, where was Scully? Had he heard?

And then in a flash, Snell whisked the blade away from the captain, grabbed Lillian, and pointed it at her throat instead.

'Untie my ma and Frank Junior!' he hollered at Matty and Jimmy. 'Captain, unless you want blood on your hands, I command you take us to the lifeboats immediately!'

'No!' Patch and Esty screamed together. And then everything seemed to happen at once. Something red hurtled through the air, landing – crack – on Frank Senior's head. The silver-topped cane flew to the floor and Frank staggered back in a daze. Lillian sprang out of the way and rushed over to Esty.

A war cry split the air as dozens of stokers burst onto the bridge, crashing into Frank Senior, wrestling him to the ground and holding him there despite his spitting and cursing.

A furious cry from Mrs Snell. A volley of swear words from Frank Senior. And then there was Scully binding Frank Senior tight to the railings, and now the stokers were cheering.

Patch looked up. Something was scuttling down the rigging like a spider. Something with a mass of black hair and one shoe.

'Captain . . .' said Patch, wrenching her eyes away.

Turo shoved the newspaper at the captain. The captain smoothed it out and read it, his whiskers twitching furiously.

'Well, WHY didn't you tell me?' boomed the captain. 'Criminals on my boat! I won't stand for it!'

'Because they were frightened, Captain Westow. What with you always encouraging the crew to hand over stowaways for grog.' It was Mrs Chilkes bustling up the stairs trailed by a crowd of open-mouthed kitchen staff.

'Thank goodness you're safe,' she said to Patch, enveloping her in a hug so fierce she almost squeezed the breath out of her.

The captain blushed and swallowed. Patch could see he was a bit in awe of Mrs Chilkes. He turned to the crew.

'Seamen! Stokers! Let's get this ship into port!

Perkins, stop looking shifty and tell the purser we need –
what d'you call them – the Manhattan Constabulary?

'The New York Police Department, sir,' chipped
in Turo.

'Yes, yes, that's it, the New York Police Department –
to take these rascals off our hands when we dock. Mrs
Chilkes, can we organise hot chocolate for everyone
and a snifter of brandy for the adults. It's a thirsty
business catching criminals!'

Turo and Lillian began to shake hands and clap
backs with the stokers. Matty and Esty gazed at each
other, arms entwined. Jimmy picked up his trombone
and struck up a tune. Sid scampered back and
forth joyously.

But someone was missing.

Someone important.

Someone with whom they could not have
done without.

On the far side of the deck, a red satin shoe
lay abandoned.

Patch cricked her neck and looked up at the mast.
Nothing there.

The ship boomed, the engines roared back into life
and they were moving again, nudging their way into
New York Harbour and towards their pier.

Where was the World's Greatest Stowaway? Had she gone? Without saying goodbye?

Patch picked up the shoe and fled.

* * *

On the upper deck, Babette was already halfway through the porthole with just her torso and her head visible.

'Babette!' Patch exclaimed. 'Were you really going to leave without saying goodbye?'

'Of course not – I knew you'd find me. And what perfect timing! I see you've brought my shoe.' She grinned. 'Can you throw my bag out after me?'

'You're not really going to drop into the sea are you? You'll drown!'

'I won't,' said Babette. Her eyes were dancing. Excitement seemed to come off her in waves. 'I told you, the longshoremen are meeting me ... their rowing boat is coming alongside just now.'

'But ... the captain wants to thank you. There's hot chocolate and brandy. Mrs Chilkes made it specially ...'

'Oh, fiddlesticks to the captain. That's right, squeeze the shoe into the bag, there should be space, and now don't forget to throw it out after me. No lily-livered throwing, mind, you have to properly hurl it.'

Babette wriggled further through the porthole. Now only her head and shoulders remained, her hands gripping the sides. 'Wait!' Her eyes gleamed. 'Come with me! I can see you are an exceptionally adventurous soul.'

And for a second Patch was tempted. But then she glanced down at the ring and it glinted on her thumb, and she knew she couldn't go anywhere because she had a jeweller's shop to get to and a mystery to resolve.

The ship boomed and Babette's eyes, following Patch's gaze, sparked, and the sparks seemed to hover in the air between them, flickering filaments, dancing towards Patch. Babette's mouth was open in a wide O. She was trying to say something. It looked like something important, but another boom – the ship's docking cry – split the air, drowning out the words, and then the porthole was empty. Nothing but cold morning air rushing in.

Patch hovered. She felt a little, inexplicable wrench in her chest.

Had Babette gone?

Quickly, she bent down and heaved up the bag– oh my, it weighed a ton! – and she wrestled it through the porthole, hurling it down just as Babette had instructed, with all her strength.

In the longshoreman's boat, bobbing about in the churning waters, unseen by Patch, Babette stood frozen. She was looking back at the ship in wonder. She opened her mouth and screamed something. But the words were lost on the wind.

And then Babette sat, her head in her hands, and wept.

The New York Tribune

March 20th, 1910

LOST AT SEA: MISSING GIRL RETURNS VICTORIOUS, AND NABS NOTORIOUS CRIMINAL FAMILY.

Friday morning before last, as the great ocean liner RMS *Glorious* docked at Pier 54, just across from West 14th Street, the New York City Police Department were summoned. Why? Because a notorious criminal family, long-wanted by Scotland Yard, had been apprehended on board. Accused of crimes including murder, theft, and intent to kidnap, the arrests were the work of three brave and resourceful children: Esme Leonard, Arturo Lopetrone and Lillian Green.

The police recovered a vast amount of

stolen goods – including several pounds of loose diamonds, a dozen fur stoles, and various pieces of extremely rare and costly jewellery – most of it sewn into the linings of the family's luggage and clothes.

It is believed the villains might have got away with their plan to set up 'shop' in New York City, if the opportunity had not presented itself to kidnap a young heiress on board, and further line their coffers. Little did they know the heiress in question, 'Lilian de Haviland,' was in fact the more humble Lillian Green, sister of Esther Green, a stewardess on the ship and no relation to the famous banking family at all. It was a fatal mistake on the Snells' part, for they hadn't reckoned on being found out by the trio of young sleuths.

The *Tribune* caught up with Miss Leonard, by all accounts the driving force of the group, on a packed Saturday night at the Treble Clef Club, where the renowned musician Jimmy Taylor dedicated his latest composition to her, an exuberant ragtime called 'Pass the Parcel.'

Sitting at the top table, surrounded by her friends, Esme – or Patch, as she prefers to be called – recounted the events of the last few days. The young lady was catapulted into adventure after boarding the ship by mistake in Liverpool. Back in the British Isles, her guardian, having no idea where she was, alerted the authorities. It was believed the child had run away. No one guessed she was on a ship halfway across the Atlantic.

'I wasn't a real stowaway because I didn't mean to hide out on the ship on purpose,' Patch was at pains to point out. 'It was an accident. As everyone knows, being a *real* stowaway takes great skill and daring.'

Accidental stowaway or not, the youngster had a good nose for sniffing out Wanted Criminals. 'I knew the Snells were up to no good the moment I laid eyes on them,' Patch confided. 'And when we found proof, we knew we had to act.' It helped that there was a considerable reward being offered. 'And I'd had a lot of practice,' she added, 'reading comics, you know, like *Girls' Best Friend*. They give you ideas.'

Was Patch enjoying her stay in New York?

'Oh yes,' she replied, nodding her head in time to the music. 'I've been to the Metropolitan Opera House to see Anna Pavlova dance *The Dying Swan* and met Mr Akeley who told me all about the dioramas he is creating in the American Museum of Natural History. But best of all was meeting up with Turo's family in Little Italy.'

Turo is a ship hand on the *Glory*. In fact, being the youngest and least experienced boy on board, he is known as 'the boots,' mainly charged with keeping the crew's quarters ship-shape. His recent endeavours, however, mean he has been promoted to steward-in-training. 'He is on course to become a captain himself by the time he is twenty-one,' said Captain Thomas Westow, who was also amongst the party at the Treble Clef. Westow was escorting a lady friend known only as Mrs Chilkes.

Were the rumours true that the world's greatest stowaway, Babette, had been on board?

Our young interviewee hesitated as if reluctant to give the game away. 'She was,' she eventually replied. 'Without her help, things could've gone very wrong.'

Patch is currently staying in the care of a stewardess at the Plaza Hotel on Fifth Avenue, but will be returning to Liverpool very soon. She will be accompanied by her friend Lillian Green, whose sister is due to marry steward Mr Matthew McKeone before the ship sets sail. 'It's so romantic,' said Patch, clasping hands with her friend Lillian who, despite her spectacles, has the air of a modern-day Alice in Wonderland.

The reward of several hundred dollars is to be split between Patch and her two friends. What will they spend the money on?

Turo claimed he would invest his in a pizza parlour 'like Lombardi's on Spring Street,' to be run by his family. Patch and Lillian hope to combine their winnings to pay for Lillian's education and board at a school in Liverpool, England. 'Then Esty and Matty can visit every time they dock,' explained Patch.

The interview drew to a close as the band swung into a final rendition of 'Pass the Parcel' and the audience filled the dance floor. We are pleased to report that young Patch Leonard was by far and away the very best dancer in the joint.

Chapter Twenty-Three

P atch loved New York: the hustle and bustle of it; the sense of excitement that hung in the air; the wide avenues, the mansions, the steel towers that stretched high into the sky. It was alive, day and night. Everywhere you looked there was something new to see: elevated train tracks, street cars, squares and parks.

June Snell had told the truth about one thing at least. Tiffany & Co., at 401 Fifth Avenue, was just as grand as she had said it was: like a Venetian palace, all white marble, and with a great clock perched on the shoulders of a giant bronze Atlas at the entrance.

It was lucky their picture had been in the papers and that they were feted by all of New York. Ordinarily, two little girls walking into a fancy jewellery shop and demanding to be told 'who, exactly who, purchased this ruby ring,' would have been given short shrift.

But on this occasion, they got their answer.

The ring, they were told by an elegant shopgirl, had been bought exactly one month previously by a woman named Elizabeth Leonard.

Patch had to sit down.

There were no seats nearby, so she sat on the white marble floor.

E. & E.

Elizabeth and Esme.

She didn't understand.

Was Elizabeth Leonard her mother?

'This means you have to come back with me!' said Lillian, her face alight. She clutched Patch's hand. 'To see Miss Alice. Ask about Elizabeth. She must know her if she left the ring with her!'

Patch looked at her friend whose future was now so certain.

Should she go back?

Did she need to know?

She'd managed perfectly well without a mother so far.

But . . .

She could see Lillian was bursting to have her for company.

She'd achieved her goal of watching Anna Pavlova dance *The Dying Swan*.

And it would be nice to sail on the *Glory* one more time.

'All right,' she said. 'I will.'

* * *

The five days at sea flew by. The shipping line was so delighted with all the publicity, they insisted the girls – and Sid, who was theirs now – sail as special guests. That meant a sumptuous cabin – called 'deluxe' in the brochure – with its own sitting room, pink blossom wallpaper, two cosy armchairs and a silk-lined dog basket by the fire. Better still, it was understood that the girls and the dog could have the run of the ship.

Patch and Lillian quickly developed a routine. When they weren't toasting marshmallows and reading out loud to one another by the fire, they spent most of their time roller skating round and round the boat deck. They had dipped into their winnings so that they could have a pair of skates each and Lillian was soon almost as good as Patch.

Every afternoon the girls had tea with the captain. They'd tramp down to the kitchen to collect a tray of tea and crumpets, and tramp back up again to tuck into it on the bridge. If the sun was out and the wind was down, they could sit for hours admiring the view as the ship churned its way homewards.

Most of the time, Turo was busy: scrubbing, painting, polishing and running errands for the senior stewards. But on the point of tea, the captain was adamant. Turo must come too. It would be a tradition, he insisted, that would continue long after the girls had gone. He liked Turo: they talked of the sea, the sea, and nothing but the sea. He admired the boy's passion and his tenacity. He saw something of himself in his new young friend.

Dinner was a sedate affair without Jimmy to liven things up. There *was* a band of course, but it didn't have the same swing. Anyway, the girls preferred to eat supper with Mrs Chilkes in the kitchen where the food was simple – a Yorkshire pudding filled with beef stew followed by a whole apple encased in sweet suet pastry – instead of things blanketed in fancy sauces and given French names.

Funnily enough, Sid was no longer hooked on ginger biscuits. Mrs Chilkes said it was a sign that he was happy now and she had taken to producing all kinds of treats – a pork chop, a piece of beef skirt, a slice of gammon – all of which Sid gobbled up with gusto.

Late in the evening the stewards and stewardesses would congregate in the tiny crew's lounge, and Matty would get his fiddle out and play joyous folk songs, and everyone would dance and sing along. Later still, the tempo would slow, and he'd sing about love and longing and gaze into Esty's eyes, as though they were bottomless pools and he was drowning in them.

After precisely five days and forty-five minutes, the ship steamed into the harbour at Liverpool. It was a breezy, bright blue day and the docks were lively, full of people waving and welcoming the ship, purchasing tickets from the bustling departure lounge, or simply enjoying the fine weather and strolling alongside the River Mersey.

On board, everyone lined up to bid farewell to the girls: the kitchen staff, the stokers, the stewards. There were hugs all round, with Turo, Scully, the captain, Mrs Chilkes and finally, Esty and Matty. But it wasn't a tearful goodbye. The ship needed to be prepared for her return journey. Five days of cleaning and painting, of stores being replenished and coal being loaded. There would be plenty of time to see each other again.

Now Patch scanned the cluster of people waiting to greet the passengers as they disembarked. Ahh! Someone was waving at them. A homely figure with a spotty handkerchief and a felt hat with a cluster of cherries on its brim.

'Mrs Blakeney!' cried Patch. 'We're here!'

The housekeeper took Lillian's cardboard suitcase, making a show of it, staggering under an imaginary weight. To Patch she said, 'You nearly gave me a heart attack, you did, running off like that. And who's this?' She bent to scratch Sid's ears and he wagged his stubby tail enthusiastically.

'This is Sid,' said Patch. Where was Miss Alice Grey? Had she not come to meet them?

'Don't fret, here she is,' said Mrs Blakeney, indicating a young woman dashing towards them wearing a neat blue dress and clamping a red-ribboned hat to her head. 'She's been tearing her hair out with worry, she has.'

'Well it wasn't *quite* as bad as that, Mrs B,' laughed the woman. She smiled widely at Patch and Lillian. 'Sorry, I had to dash to pick up a telegram. But I'm here now. I'm Alice and I'm guessing you're Patch.' She squeezed Patch's shoulder encouragingly. 'And Lillian! I'm so happy to see you again!'

'Well,' said Alice after they had all shaken hands, 'shall we walk back? And while we go, you can tell me all about your adventures, not missing anything out and starting from the beginning.'

As they walked and talked, Patch kept glancing at Alice. She had such a merry face. She had taken her hat off now, because holding it in place was too much bother, and her hair didn't look *at all* like it had been nearly torn out. It was the shiniest hair Patch had ever seen, the colour of wheat, twisted up like a rope and coiled neatly on top of her head. Her eyes, a tweedy blend of greyish green, were kind. And she was the sort of person you felt like you had known for years after only five minutes.

As they made their way along the winding streets that wriggled their way up towards the school, Alice asked all the right questions and listened intently as Patch and Lillian related their tale, only interrupting once.

'Patch,' Alice broke in gently. They had reached a crossroads on the corner of which stood a little sweet shop with a smartly striped awning.

'Before we go any further, I think an apology might be in order. I found this.' Alice handed Patch her little purse, still containing a few coins from Mr Ringe. 'I understand there was a bit of a mix-up regarding some toffee. I think there's enough in there to settle up, don't you?'

* * *

The rooms at the top of the school were just as homely as Patch remembered. A small fire burned busily in the grate and there was a plate of meringues and cream on the table.

'I didn't mean to steal it,' said Patch, slipping off the ruby ring. 'It fitted on my thumb so perfectly and I forgot to take it off before I went exploring.'

Alice smiled and shook her head.

'It's yours anyway.'

Patch felt something bloom deep inside her chest. It *was* hers! The ring had felt right because it *was* right.

'But . . .' said Patch. She still needed to ask about the initials. Find out if Elizabeth was . . . But something told her to wait. And so she did, watching patiently as Alice sprang up and dug about on the mantelpiece, amongst the clutter of shells, and conkers and little vases of flowers, until she found what she was looking for – a letter written in emerald green ink on fine paper.

'You were meant to get this when I gave you the ring.'

'Oh!'

'Read it,' said Alice gently.

Patch took the letter, her heart thumping nineteen to the dozen.

Dear Esme,

I have longed and longed to write to you. I hope that now you are twelve you may be wise enough and old enough to understand. I am sorry to have left you. But my feet do not like to stay still. I tried it but I couldn't manage. I have my freedom but my heart often feels broken. I hope you will accept this ring with my love and that one day you will forgive me.

From your mother,
Elizabeth

Patch stared at Alice. *My feet do not like to stay still.* Something almost unbelievable was slotting into place.

'Does . . . Elizabeth use another name?'

'Yes,' said Alice softly. Her eyes were glistening, like mossy pebbles after a heavy bout of rain.

'Is it . . . Babette?'

Alice nodded. 'You look very similar,' she said, reaching out to smooth Patch's wayward hair.

Patch moved over to the big picture window as if in a dream.

Babette! Her mother?

She didn't know whether to laugh or cry. It was true that Babette had always been there when she'd needed help. When Frank Junior had ambushed her, when he'd thrown her overboard, and right at the end when Frank Senior had been felled with her red satin shoe.

And there had been that lullaby, the one about the waves and the water; it had reminded Patch of . . . something so long ago. And her touch. The red-hot hand, her fierce, kind words, and those sparks that seemed to fly out of her eyes and settle, so warm and true, on Patch's skin. There *had* been a connection, Patch could see that now.

'Patch,' said Alice. It was as if her voice was coming from far away, so full was Patch's head with images and memories. Lillian reached out and squeezed her hand.

'We were at school together, your mother and I, and she has been in touch with me throughout her career,' explained Alice, saying the word 'career' so kindly, without a trace of irony. 'Mr Ringe would write to me of your progress, and I would pass it on. But it was always Elizabeth who sent the instructions. She was here a week or two before the *Glorious* set sail and that's when she asked if you could come and live with me, Patch. I was more than happy to oblige. Elizabeth is my dear, dear friend.'

Patch slipped the ruby ring back onto her thumb. Babette had tried to tell her something right at the end. Had she seen the ring? Had she known?

'Patch!' said Lillian, and her eyes were wide. 'Oh ... what's that word? Can you believe how *serendipitous* it was that you managed to get yourself stuck on the very same boat that your mother decided to stow away on!'

'Well done, Lillian, that *is* the perfect word,' said Alice.

'As if it was *meant* to happen,' said Lillian. 'Oh, Patch ...'

'And,' said Alice, 'this came today.' She fished something out of her pocket. 'The telegram I collected earlier. It's addressed to me but I think the contents apply to you. Would you like to read it?'

Patch took it. Her hand was shaking so much that the words danced up and down.

'Shall I?' said Lillian.

'Yes please,' said Patch.

Alice. I have met my darling
girl, Esme! But I didn't realise
it was her until it was too
late. If she finds her way back
to you, please keep her safe.
Tell her I am sorry and I will
understand if she never wants to
see me again. Your ever-loving
friend, Elizabeth.

'But ...' If Patch was her darling girl, why had she run away?

'She thought she would have been a terrible mother, Patch,' said Alice. 'She couldn't keep still. A square peg, everyone always called her – a square peg in a round hole.'

A square peg in a round hole. *Like me*, thought Patch.

Lillian regarded Patch solemnly. 'Are you going to leave us now?'

Was she?

The safest thing would be to stay with Alice and Lillian and Mrs Blakeney, who was a bit like Mrs Chilkes. She'd receive an education. She'd be looked after. She'd have the pleasure of being with her friend.

But at the same time she could feel that her feet were already starting to itch inside her boots.

Did her mother want her?

She remembered how, right at the end, when she'd been half in and half out of the porthole, Babette had asked Patch if she wanted to go with her. What had she said? 'I can see you are an exceptionally adventurous soul.'

Outside Patch could see the masts and the twinkle of water. Her heart ached. For movement. For adventure. For the blazing star that was her mother.

Before she could change her mind, she rushed into the bedroom and rummaged around in her bag for her skates. She found her reward money, left half for Lillian and tucked the rest into her pocket.

And then she was back in the cosy room, with the rosy apple walls and the flickering firelight. Lillian and Alice were talking quietly by the bookshelf. 'Have you read this? Have you read that?'

And now there was no question. She could feel the wanderlust in her veins, fizzing and spitting. Her mother's blood. Calling her, calling her.

'I'm just going out for a quick skate,' she said. They turned and she knew they knew, and sadness filled the room.

But there was something else, too.

Hope. Encouragement. Understanding.

And then she was racing down the stairs and Sid was standing at the top, barking. She paused and they looked at each other, and he grunted and she said, 'Do you want to come, too?' and he barked 'yes.' And then she was buckling up her skates and swooping through the winding streets, wind streaming through her hair, skirt billowing, Sid scampering along beside her.

They didn't know it yet, but ahead of them, down by the docks, a second vessel was nudging its way into the harbour.

And there on the top deck stood a piratical figure, tall and proud, by the ship's bow.

A mass of black hair. An indigo dress. Scarlet shoes.

It was the World's Greatest Stowaway.

She was wild and she was fearless, and she had come back for her daughter.

She would fight for her if she had to.

There would be no more 'instructions'. No more being passed from pillar to post.

She watched now as Sid and Patch appeared, the dog scampering, the girl skating, both of them moving with utter determination. She could see that they both knew, with all their hearts, that they were doing the right thing.

They stopped.

They had seen the ship.

They had seen her.

Tears streamed down Babette's face. It was the greatest good fortune. A miracle.

She raised a hand and waved.

Patch waved back fiercely. Sid ran round and round in happy circles.

Soon, very soon, they would be together again.

Acknowledgements

To Alice Swan, my esteemed editor at Faber. Thank you × a million for trusting me to turn such a skimpy idea into a full blown story. And then (your special magic) knowing how to turn it into an even better story!

Also at Faber: Natasha Brown, Bethany Carter, Ama Badu, Emma Eldridge, Sarah Lough (goodbye and good luck!) and Kellie Balseiro, thank you for taking the very best care of my books. Thank you to Maurice Lyon for the kindest, most encouraging copy editing. To Kim Geyer for your wonderful illustrations, always full of joie de vivre and always spot on.

To agents old and new: Tessa David, it was an absolute joy and a pleasure working with you. Lucy

Irvine, thank you for welcoming me so warmly into your fold.

To Heather, Lis, Tim and Graham. We didn't get to meet much over the last year but when we did it was invaluable.

To Ben in Year 9, for greeting me every day with a cheery 'one day less until publication!'

Finally Nick, Poppy and Rose. This book was written during lockdown and for a short while we were all thrown together: carving out our work spaces, grappling with Zoom, Teams and all the rest. It was a weird and surreal time, but all the better for being with you. You are brilliant, and I love you.